LOVE'S HOPE

JA'NESE DIXON

For more information address:

Purpose Prevails Publishing
2231B Center St. STE 144
Deer Park, TX 77536
www.purposeprevailspublishing.com

Special discounts are available on quantity purchases. For details contact the publisher at the address above.

First Edition ISBN-13: 978-0-9987811-1-2 (paperback)

First Trade Paperback Printing: July 2017

Printed in the United States of America

Love never gives up, never loses faith,
is always hopeful, and endures
through every circumstance.
1 Corinthians 13:7

CONTENTS

SNEAK PEEK BOOK 1: CARAMEL SURPRISE

SNEAK PEEK BOOK 3: HIDDEN DESIRE

Can she find hope when all else fails?

Sandra James has life all figured out, or so she thinks. But her successful business, commitment-averse boyfriend, and her sister's shotgun wedding threaten her health and sanity. She will run to Love Never Fails Retreat in hopes of relinquishing her childhood dreams and embracing her reality even if it breaks her heart.

LOVE'S HOPE is an inspirational romantic novella set in a small Texas ranch that you can read as a stand-alone or as part of the series.

RUNNING

"*I* broke it off."

Sandra clicked the blinker to signal her lane change. Traffic was the usual, parking lot. Houston citizens didn't care about her grief-stricken attempt to put as much space between herself and the city, as humanly possible. The drivers showed no love, and neither did her life.

"What?" Bruce asked.

"Are you serious?" Sandra yelled at the Honda acting like an Escalade. She slammed on her brakes. *Why did they refuse to merge nicely?*

"Sandi, what's up with you?"

Sandra let out the pent up air held captive in her lungs. She wished she could explain. But she didn't have an answer because it was a list of incidents all neatly packaged to drive her insane. Her life. Her sister. The wedding. It was all too much. Too soon.

"Jerk!" She laid on the horn.

"Sandi pull over." His command filled the cabin of her SUV.

The tears rolling down her cheeks didn't compare to those puddled in her eyes. They made it hard to see. Her grip on the steering wheel tightened, and for the first time all day she was grateful. The traffic slowed from a crawl to a stop. The parking lot called Highway 45 meant she would not harm herself or anyone else.

So she let the tears fall until her shoulders shook and Bruce held the line, she could feel him absorbing her pain.

"What is it? Please, Sandi, answer me."

The horn from the truck behind her jarred her attention. Traffic was moving once again. She lifted her foot from the pedal and rolled forward.

"Sweet Sandi, pull over," Bruce said, coaxing her with his secret weapon, a nickname he'd sing to her from time to time to the tune of *Sweet Sadie*.

"Oh...oh okay," she stated as she gasped for air. Nodding as if Bruce could see her.

Bruce released her barriers. She couldn't hold anything from him. It was always a safe place. A place she needed, space where she could cry, whine, question, or even doubt if she wanted without judgment. She didn't have to be Sandra with an "S" on her chest; she was plain ole Sandi. No airs. No pretense.

"I wish you were here," she stated shifting the gear to park on the shoulder of the highway. She heard Bruce mumbling to someone in the room, Sandra figured she called during a recording session and it made her feel worse.

"Are you in a session? I'm so sorry—"

"Not anymore, and don't apologize."

"Bruce, I'm sorry for disrupting you, I don't know what came over me. But I'm better." She wiped the tears away, willing herself to pull it together.

His lingering silence made her ramble on.

"I...I...," she took another deep breath, "I just don't know what to do anymore."

Sandra watched the cars moving past. They must have removed the accident off the highway, she thought, as the cars picked up speed. She was content to sit and watch them disappear into the horizon.

She heard a door close and his keys jingling, followed by the chirp of Bruce disarming his car alarm. He was in Atlanta and the first person she thought to call. She hoped she wouldn't regret it.

"Spill it," he said with a solid thump of the door closing.

It was silent. Sandra felt like a fool for crying and losing it.

"5...4...3.... Don't make me get to one woman or I'll jump on the first thing smoking to Houston," he said.

She laughed. The countdown always helped.

"Cindy is pregnant."

They sat in their cars in the silence. Bruce knew how to give her space to process her thoughts.

"I'm...I'm happy for her and Russell. I can't wait for the wedding and the babies too." She tried to smile, but her face wouldn't cooperate.

"Babies?" He emphasized.

She nodded and realized he couldn't see her. "Huh,

yes," she wiped her nose with the side of her hand, "twins." The last word was released with a squeak because the tears had returned.

"Breathe Sandi."

She nodded again and followed his advice. She had to pull it together.

"Where are you and where are you going?"

She heard the engine turn over on his end.

"Don't come. I'm better now I just needed to say it aloud. I'm better. Promise."

Sandra searched her glove compartment for a tissue. She pushed the items left and right slamming it closed. Then she looked in her car door and found a napkin from the shop.

Pulling down her visor she groaned...

"A blotchy mess," he said, humor hanging on every word. Then he laughed and so did she. Bruce's laughter soothed the ache threatening to break her.

"I hate you right now."

They laughed more. Bruce was right. Sandra was a blotchy mess. Thank God for waterproof eyeliner and mascara. She used the hard napkin to clean herself up. Flipping the visor closed, she decided it was time to get back on the highway.

"So Cindy is pregnant with twins, and her wedding is less than a year away—"

"Correction, they moved the date up. We have less than two months." His accuracy in recounting the demands on her time was impeccable.

"Two months? Are you still planning it? How can you? You have too much on your plate."

"Don't get me started again. My mascara can only take one meltdown a day."

Their laughter filled the car. That was why she called him.

"And where does Alonso fit into this scenario?"

She knew she couldn't slide that one pass him. Her boyfriend, correction, ex-boyfriend wanted to play house and told her he had no plans of getting married anytime soon. Her vision was cloudy again.

Sandra wiped away the tears, taking deep breathes. It was over.

"I can't stay in a relationship not headed to marriage," she stated. Not to mention her "Get Married" deadline was approaching. And there went her "Start a Family" goal too.

"So are the tears for him?"

Sandra shook her head, "No." Alone in her SUV. Sitting in traffic. She knew she looked a mess. She thought about the source of her pain. Was it the shock of finally ending it with Alonso? She knew they were nearing the end even if they both didn't want to admit it. Maybe it was the thought of starting over? Or knowing the tears are...

"Sandi answer me..."

She took a deep inhale through the nose she released a very audible breath from her mouth. She could do this.

"No, Bruce. I know it won't work between us, but I hoped it would. I wanted it to. I just fault myself for letting it linger longer than it should have. The tears are because, hold on," she took the first exit she saw.

Sandra pulled into the Walmart-size gas station and located a parking space under a light. Again she placed the car in park. She looked around, and it was well lit, and she had another hour before the sun completely set.

"The tears Bruce are my way of letting go of it all. My dream," she whispered, "I can't find a husband. This means I can't have kids. This means I won't have a family. And I will live my life alone. And I just—"

"Really Sandi? You break up with the man for five minutes, and now you're an old maid."

"It's not funny."

She could see the smile on his face in Atlanta from Houston. The octave of his voice went higher when he smiled. And she smiled with him, lessening the hurt. A little.

"And to see Cindy get it all," she continued, "I'm happy for her really." She realized she must sound pathetic. It was her sister. Her baby sister at that. She was happy for her. However, she couldn't help but compare their lives.

Cindy planned to marry her high school sweetheart who now played for the Houston Texans. While Sandra owned Coffee Confessions, a little slice of her heaven on earth.

The cafe served coffee and light food accompanied by a bookshop and intimate concerts. The business turned a profit every year, with great employees, customers, and a boyfriend until a few hours ago.

When would her someday come...

"Sandi, you have to stop comparing. You are two

different people. You wanted a different life. Be patient, your time will come."

As always, he read her mind. She hated him. Not really. But she kind of did when he did that.

"I know. I know. I guess I'm tired and need to regroup. I am going to spend the week with Serafine."

"That sounds better. Do you need me to come down and cover things at the cafe?"

"No. My staff can cover it. What would I look like having you fly in to cover my business when I'm taking you away from your clients now?

"You would look like a friend in need of a hand. It's all good."

"I appreciate the offer. But it's not necessary. I have a great crew, and I'm only a phone call away." And she did. They made life much easier for her.

"Good. You sound better already."

"I love visiting her."

"Well, you need to get going. I don't want you driving on those backroads at night."

"Yes, father," she said laced with sarcasm. They laughed again.

"Ha ha ha... Alright, Kevin Hart. Get going and call me when you get there."

Sandra sat up and put her seatbelt back on. She wanted to make it before dark too. The country roads leading to Loving Ranch were lined with acres and acres of trees. They made for a beautiful sight during the day but became a black hole at night.

"I will. And Bruce..."

"Yeah..."

"Thank you."

"You're welcome. Get to Serafine's and call me. And Sandi, don't give up. You have to believe God has something better heading your way. I believe it."

"I'm tired of waiting. Maybe it's not for me, and I need to accept it." Her voice did not sound as confident as she hoped.

"Don't sound like that. Here's what I'll do. I'll believe enough both of us. Now get going and no more cryin' and driving. Okay?"

"Okay."

"Love you," he said as his warmth filled her with courage.

"Back at ya kid!"

They disconnected with the rumble of his laughter lingering as she reentered the highway. Sandra didn't share Bruce's optimism, at least not yet, but she thanked God for him. He was the best friend a girl could have.

Before backing out of the parking space, she bowed her head for a quick prayer.

Father,

> *Help me use this time to let go of what is not for me.*
> *Help me to see and embrace your plan for me.*

> *In Jesus' name, Amen.*

With that, she put in KB's CD. Traffic appeared lighter. Serafine's retreat had perfect timing. She would enjoy the ride tonight and use the week to uncover a different future for herself. Maybe she was called to live her life single.

No husband.

No kids.

Those thoughts felt like a burden she could not carry. She did not want to carry. And every inch of her being wanted to deny it. But could she when the evidence of her life made it almost blatantly clear.

Sandra could feel the tears threatening to reemerge. Her thumb lingered over the up arrow to increased the volume, hoping to drown out the sound of her breaking heart. And she heard a chime of an incoming text.

She glanced at the display, it was Alonso.

We need to talk about this. Call me. Love you.

HER DILEMMA

Sandra turned off the paved country road to the gravel path, she passed through the gates. The wooden welcome sign read "Loving Ranch." She knew she still had a mile or two until she reached the Josephine Retreat Center. She exhaled her relief of making it before nightfall. She tapped the display to pause her music. Driving the distance at a slow crawl. She could hear the gravel crunching under the weight of her SUV.

Jojo's Journey was the main street that ran the entire property. It was lined with trees and wide enough for two lanes. But without a distinct line separating the lanes most drivers road in the middle. The trees seemed to draw closer as the sun continued its departure. They were close enough to almost touch. Sandra's eyes darting from left to right on deer watch. She'd experience more than one scare with deer on the property.

Serafine instructed her to go to the center, with her tight grip on the steering wheel. Sandra allowed her eyes to veer from the path for a moment to look at the sky just above the trees. They looked like a bed of green clouds kissing the subtle traces of light left by the sun, taking its warmth with it. Her left hand lifted the buttons to close her windows. She was enjoying the fresh air, but the sun's departure caused a slight chill to linger in the air.

Sandra cleared the bend at a slow speed and saw the lights ahead. She could also see Serafine in a rocking chair on the porch. Sandra smiled at seeing her college friend. They did not take enough time to visit one another. She was excited about the next week on the ranch with her.

Serafine must have heard her approaching, she stood smiling and waved her towards the fellowship hall. Sandra waved back and returned her big as Texas smile. She parked between the center and the fellowship hall. Sandra turned off her ignition and jumped out leaving her door wide open. She ran to grab ahold of her friend, her sister.

"Sissy...," they said it in unison.

Laughter mixed with tears of joy. They stood in the parking lot in a strong embrace. She could feel the strain of Houston exiting her body as she held Serafine close. The small circles she rubbed on her back relaxed Sandra further, and the tears resurfaced.

The stars overhead and the night's silence held only traces of God's nature basking in His offering. A ringing from her phone required her to break their embrace.

"Just a sec...," Sandra brushed her tears away with a swipe of her index finger. She retraced her steps with a slight jog. The ringing through her speakers was thunderous against the quietness of her surroundings.

She looked at the display, it was Bruce. She hopped in and pressed to activate the call.

"Hey, you. Are you there?"

"Yes, I made it a few minutes ago. I hit a patch of construction, but I'm here now." She leaned across and grabbed her purse from the floor of the back seat. She tossed Serafine a quick finger, signaling she needed a moment.

Serafine mouthed, *I'll be on the porch*. Sandra acknowledged her with a slight nod. And she watched Serafine reclaim her seat.

"Great," Bruce's voice brought her back to gathering her belongings. She removed her journal from the center console. She removed her keys and sent him to her wireless headset. She tossed her worn journal, phone, and keys into her purse on the driver's seat and went to the back to grab her luggage.

"I'm not going to keep you," he continued, "I wanted to make sure you reached your destination in one piece. Are you feeling better? Driving usually helps."

"I am." She removed her bags and closed the lift. "It feels good to be here again. When is the last time you been out here?" She pulled the oversized bag across the gravel. She walked not bothering to engage her alarm or lock her truck doors.

"Years. Tell Serafine I said 'Hello'."

Sandra reached the porch, "Bruce says 'Hey'."

Serafine sat rocking with a lap quilt tucked around her legs responded, "Tell him, 'Long time no see'" and went back to knitting with a smile.

Bruce hearing Serafine responded and told Sandra, "Tell her I'll come by soon."

"I'll tell her, but let me call you back. I want to get these bags inside and get settled in." She disconnected the call and joined Serafine in a rocker adjacent to hers. She breathed in the night air and watched the moon's reflection dance on the lake. They sat for a few moments with only the silence holding the space between them.

"Thank you for coming," Serafine broke the silence, "I hate to ask, but I had to decide between increasing my staff or offering more scholarships. And I chose the latter."

"Hush girl! You are offering me some much-needed downtime, and I'm glad you asked. You are doing a great thing out hear." She gestured with her hand at the property. Their eyes held and Sandra could see relief reflected in her sister's eyes. But they also looked tired. It made her wonder if there was more Serafine was not saying.

"When is the last time you had a good night's sleep?"

Serafine looked away and placed her knitting and quilt on the seat of the rocker. "Let me help you with this luggage since you packed for a month and not a week."

Sandra laughed with her. "Now you know I don't pack light. And I'll let you dodge my question...for now." She grabbed Serafine's hand and give if a supportive squeeze.

"Thank you."

THE TWO SUCCESSFULLY TOOK THE luggage into her room. Then met back on the porch with sweet tea, sandwiches, and chips. Sandra didn't realize until she took the first bite how hungry she was. Thinking back over her day she recalled breakfast at the cafe but her lunch break was cut short by a larger than usual, lunch rush and her sister's call.

"Are you ready to talk shop?" Serafine intersected her daydreaming.

"Sure." She dusted the crumbs on her hands over her plate. Serafine walked back inside and returned with another sandwich. She smiled at her friend and unwrap it giving Serafine her full attention.

"This week is one of my more exclusive retreats. It is not open to the public. All of the attendees are either repeats, or they are referrals."

"Referrals from whom?" Sandra said before taking a big bite of the turkey sandwich with extra pickles and onions. Her friend knew just how she liked it.

"It varies. Pastors. Mentors. Friends. Sometimes counselors too. I don't have an actual policy as to how they learn about it other than it must be based on prior experience with this particular retreat."

"Do you have the same requirement with all of your retreats?" She asked before taking a drink of her tea.

"No. They are listed on our website and quarterly newsletter. I sometimes run small ads in conference programs from time to time. But that is rare. I normally having a waiting list, so I don't advertise unless the conference reaches out to me."

"Okay. So what makes this retreat different and what will you need me to do?"

Sandra sat and listened as Serafine explained the Love Never Fails Retreat. It was held annually for groups and privately as requested. She shared that it differed due to its intensity and that many of the participants had life-altering circumstances, which required stronger content and tough love.

"But don't you do that always?" She asked nibbling on a chocolate chip cookie.

"Of course, but there are limits to how much I can push during my weekend retreats. This retreat is for a full week, and I have had prior phone sessions with most of the ladies. Therefore, when they get here we can hit the ground running."

Serafine explained the weekend schedule and session format. Sandra listened and thought back to her sister, Alonso and the cafe. The week would allow her a much-needed pause, to halt life. For the past few years, she found herself running nonstop. She opened and closed the cafe nearly every day. Especially since Bruce relocated to Atlanta. And adding to the mix, her duties as the wedding planner for Cindy left Sandra strained and burnt out. She really needed to learn how to say no.

"Give words to your thoughts," Serafine cut into her thoughts.

She was embarrassed to be caught. But she could see the concern in Serafine's eyes.

"I'm sorry. Things just got complicated fast, and I am not handling it well."

"Hold that thought, I have a something for you." She walked inside letting the screen door slam behind her.

Sandra finished off her tea and closed her eyes as her headrest on the chair. She rocked with a slight moment of her crossed feet. She wanted the soothing motion to cure the aches lingering in her heart. But she felt them hovering as she took several deep breathes. She knew she could be honest with Serafine. However, she did not know if she was ready to give words to the envy and discontentment infiltrating her heart towards her sister.

Serafine returned with another slam of the screen door.

"Now you know Miss Jo would have her tail for lunch for slamming that screen door like that." The warmth of Serafine's laugh and soft footsteps brought a smile to her face. Sandra opened her eyes as Serafine thrust a gift bag in her direction.

She took the offering with a soft, "Thank you."

Sandra placed the bag in her lap. She was surprised by the gesture, although she knew she shouldn't be. Serafine was the most giving person she knew. Serafine would give down to her last without blinking an eye. It was who she was.

Serafine reclaimed her chair with a smile.

Sandra scrambled through her memories of her childhood friend to find the right words to express it and landed on chameleon. Serafine was like a chameleon. She knew how to shape and mold herself to be exactly what people needed.

"What is this?" Sandra asked. She touched the bag and glanced down but only saw white tissue paper. She lifted to gauge the weight. It felt heavy.

"Open it." A mischievous smile crossed Serafine's face.

Sandra pushed the tissue paper aside and pulled out a clear package. She placed the gift bag on the floor. It was fabric and colorful. She noticed a card attached with a pretty purple bow.

Sandra read aloud, "A friend loves at all times. Proverbs 17:17." She put the card in the bag and removed the plastic to find a beautiful quilt.

When did she become a weeping willow? She felt overwhelmed by her generosity. She was providing her refuge and still felt compelled to give her a beautiful gift.

Sandra opened it as wide as her arms would allow. Running her hand over the delicate stitching. She saw fabric with little coffee beans, and mugs. There were pops of teal and soft tan covering most of the quilt. It was finished with a rich royal purple binding.

"Did you make this?" Sandra asked not wanting to take her eyes off the masterpiece in her lap. But she did for a brief moment to see Serafine's keen eyes peaking into her soul.

"Yes, it's a late birthday gift. I hope it will keep you warm and you'll think of me often." Again she smiled reaching for Serafine's hand, "What's going on with you? I've seen more tears from you tonight than I have in all the years I've known you."

Sandra shrugged directing her attention to her lap. It was easier to look at the beauty of it than to examine the messiness of her life.

"I'm listening," Serafine offered.

Sandra looked out on the lake and accepted her friend's most precious offering, a listening ear. Sandra started with the shop overtaking her life followed by her sister's wedding and pregnancy announcement. And rounded it all off by the on-again, off-again, relationship with Alonso. Serafine listened asking questions along the way. Sandra answered and continued filling her friend in on all the details without shame or embarrassment, and made her very heavy load a little lighter.

"My oh my, what a colorful life you lead."

"If only it was as beautiful as this quilt." Her chuckle absorbed by the cold night air. She adjusted her quilt to cover her from her shoulders to her feet. Sandra tucked it under her thighs. She could sleep in that very spot, she thought.

"Sandi, I think you should join the ladies this week. You don't have to, but you may find it useful to sit in on the sessions. I believe it will help you and your dilemma?"

"My dilemma?" Sandra asked.

"Yes, ma'am, your dilemma."

"I feel like I'm about to get the squeeze here," she said eying Serafine suspiciously, "What are you talking about?"

"No squeeze. I just see your situation from a different perspective. And stop looking at me like that." She tossed a crumbled napkin at Sandra hitting her on the forehead.

"I can't believe you just did that!"

They squealed in laughter. Sandra picked it up, tossing it back.

Once their laughter subsided, Serafine continued, "Sandi, the more I inhabit this space I see life differently." Her hand gestured to the land before them. "And the more I serve I learn God is greater than any trial we face."

"But this has nothing to do with God," Sandra said.

Serafine looked her in the eyes and said, "God abides in all things, and anything concerning His children concerns Him. And you, my sister, are His child."

Her emphasis on "all things" caused a chill to run through Sandra. How had she not considered that? She would have to think about it later. Sandra was not prepared to take the conversation further. Instead, she segued to Serafine.

"Your turn."

"Okay. But before I do, I want you to consider something. Do you trust God?"

Silence again settled between the two as they sat wrapped in their quilts. Sandra loved God. She knew who He was, she believed. But the reality of circumstances made answering the question harder than it should have been. Her growing agitation with Cindy and Alonso and her lack of satisfaction in her cafe, although she loved her employees and customers made Sandra question everything. She felt like she was on the brink of a breakdown.

"Do you think that is my problem? My lack of trust towards God." She asked with her anxiety etched on her face. She honestly did want to hear Serafine's response. She just wanted it to all go away. She came to rest and move on. Not be examined.

"Listen, you are free to do what you want," she said reading Sandra's face with the ease of a lifelong friendship. "However, I believe you could find some clarity if you give yourself room to explore what's going on in that head of yours."

Serafine stood and grabbed their glasses and dishes. She took them inside leaving Sandra with her thoughts. When Serafine returned, she sat on the edge of the table between their chairs. She faced Sandra with her hands clasped in her lap.

"There are realities of who God is that I did not learn in all my years of attending church," Serafine said and paused as if calling on the lake to help with the right words to say. "This week it could open your eyes to more about who He is outside a church. And about Jesus who wants to be the center of your life."

"I came to help you. Not give you another person with more problems."

"I believe this will be helpful for both of us. You and I talk, but I realize you know very little about the services I provide here. How about instead of helping me this weekend you participate as a retreater?"

Sandra didn't respond.

"It is up to you. You have until tomorrow morning. Early registration for Inner Circle Sisters begins at 7:00 am."

Serafine stood and place a kiss on her forehead.

"I'm inviting you to join us. But the decision is up to you."

IT'S COMPLICATED

*S*andra opened her eyes and scanned the room. *Where was she?* She sat up and noticed the quilt and thought back, relief washing over her. She recalled arriving at the ranch last night, and she'd have to thank Serafine for her quilt again. She stretched her arms over her head and rolled her shoulders. The bed wasn't like home, but she slept like a baby.

Serafine gave her a private room since was visiting as a worker instead of a retreater. Most of her guest shared rooms, she said to help them process the information and get to know one another. But Sandra was thankful for the privacy.

She reached for her phone. It was 3:45. She beat her alarm by fifteen minutes. That made her smile. Her locked phone screen displayed no missed phone calls or text messages. Good, no fires, she thought. She was free to begin her day.

Sandra tossed back the quilt and immediately

missed its warmth. What she wanted was a good strong cup of coffee. And maybe a bag of donut holes. She was certain she would find the coffee, since Serafine was a coffee lover too, but daily donuts would have to wait until she returned home.

Sandra slid on her fuzzy socks and made her way to the kitchenette. In no time she found the filters, coffee, and fixings for her coffee. She added the water, coffee grains and in minutes was rewarded with the smell of fresh coffee. She made a large deposit in her sleep deprivation. She couldn't remember the last time she'd slept more than four hours straight.

She poured her first cup of coffee and took it back to bed. Grabbing her iPad, she got back under the quilt and began her morning routine—Tasks and To-Dos.

Sandra tapped in her iPad to open her calendar and reminders. She always reviewed her daily and weekly schedules to stay on top of things. She took a long sip of the Folgers and thanked her girl for stocking her room with a coffeemaker. It wasn't her usual latte, but it was good to revisit an old favorite.

Over the next few minutes she composed emails, she followed up with vendors for Cindy's wedding, and she made a note to contact possible locations for the baby registry.

Babies.

Sandra and Cindy met yesterday for their weekly visit about the wedding progress. They did it over lunch. Sandra arrived early, and Cindy arrived late. Sandra had a rolling checklist, a paper wedding planner, invitation samples and cards for the cater, florist, and photographer. Cindy strolled in with her designer shades, perfect makeup, and red bottom shoes, she always seemed to have the world waiting on her hand and foot. But that was her Cindy Poo.

The meeting hit its marks. They covered all the decisions she needed to sign off on. They even examined the budget, then the conversation shifted.

"What's up baby sis?" Sandra asked taking another bite of her fajita chicken salad.

Sandra noticed for the first time Cindy's puffy red eyes. She pushed aside her plate and reached for Cindy's hand.

"I'm pregnant."

Sandra felt a hush move over the room. It was as if the entire restaurant paused with her statement. Or maybe it was just her. She looked out over the room and noticed the waitress picking up a napkin and chatting with little girl in the next booth over. But for some reason she could not hear the girls giggles over the blood rushing in her ears. Her heart beating faster than it was moments before. She slipped her hands free and ran them down her pants to wipe away some of the moisture.

Cindy snapped her fingers in front of Sandra's face. "Sandi are you listening."

"Really?" The snap brought her back. She saw Cindy's mouth moving but she didn't hear what she said beyond, "I'm pregnant."

The rest of their lunch and her day was a blur. She was sure she congratulated her sister. Hadn't she?

Sandra questioned her response all day. She walked

around the cafe like something from "The Walking Dead." She spoke to customers, worked with her staff but the thought of her sister having it all bombarded her entire being.

Sandra felt the tears rolling down her cheek and landing in her coffee cradled in her lap. She placed the mug on the end table and noticed the time. It was 4:27.

"Get it together girl," she said.

Wiping the tears with a Kleenex, she thought about Serafine's offer to participate in the retreat. She did not feel she needed counseling. She could not explain her response. Her tears. Nor the shift in her heart.

For some odd reason, it hurt with a constant ache to know she had nothing while Cindy had everything.

She loved her sister. She would do anything for her to the point of planning an extravagant wedding for nearly a thousand guests. But in the solitude of her private room, she allowed herself to admit, just once, for a mere second that she was envious of Cindy.

The realization made her silent tears increase their flow. Alone she let herself cry. Just this once.

After what felt like an eternity her well had run dry. She had no more tears to shed. She resigned to do what she'd always done, support her sister. She would plan the extravagant wedding with the best of the best as if it was her own.

Sandra smiled at remembering her day going from not so good to better when she decided to seek shelter. She texted Serafine her acceptance to help for the week. She canceled her appointments, prepped her staff and hightailed it to Loving Ranch.

Sandra went to the bathroom and washed her face. She declared to her reflection, "No more crying." She hoped her heart would comply.

She walked back into her room searching for the retreat schedule. She wasn't fully onboard for participating, but she wasn't adamantly against it either. She located the schedule next to her purse and a large postcard size flyer. Across the top is read, Retreater's Commandments.

"Leave it to Serafine to have commandments."

Sandra sat on the edge of the bed and skimmed the flyer. She chuckled as the commandments mimicked the ten commandments from the Bible complete with King James English. She made it to number seven and paused...Thou shall not cleave to thous phone. It even had a footnote. "Commit to being unplugged for the week. Better yet decide to turn it off after texting one final person. Remind them of your location and give them our landline number."

"She must be crazy," Sandra said to the empty room.

She considered, who would be her final person to text. She could text her mother, father, sister or even Alonso. *Ugh.*

Sandra still did not respond to his text from the night before. She was done with him and his lack of commitment. How did she expect to get married when she had a boyfriend—correction ex-boyfriend—who had no inclination towards marriage.

She sighed.

She would take a shower and get dressed. The decision would come to her. Sandra glanced at the clock. That would give her about 15 minutes to text her contact if she planned to participate.

Sandra will rub her chest relieving the tension her pent up air caused. Her life was complicated. Too complicated to solve in a week. But she trusted Serafine. She only wondered what Serafine meant by last night's question.

What did trusting God have to do with her life falling apart? She believed in God. She was a Christian but she never quite figured out what to do between Monday and Saturday except being a good person. Trying not to swear. And she was far from remaining pure. Maybe that's why she didn't have a husband.

Her Grandma Mae and Miss Josephine always warned them about giving away their milk and apparently Alonso wasn't interested in buying a cow. She laughed at her analogy.

What did she have to lose?

Nothing worth holding on to. Sandra knew she would help Serafine and she had to stay the week to do it. Which meant she could do both. Right?

Sandra scanned the schedule once more. She would do it. She would participate as long as Serafine would let her help too.

Serafine's normal co-facilitator left the country on a family emergency and Sandra knew what it was like to be without her right hand. She'd felt that way every since Bruce left the shop.

Bruce brought a smile to her face and it eased the throbbing ache in her chest. He'd text him. He would be her final contact. That settled it.

The clock read 4:29.

Sandra jumped to her feet, she hated being off schedule. She gathered her toiletries and rushed back to the bathroom. She'd shower then find Serafine.

4:53.

Sandra walked out of the bathroom balancing her clothes in a bundle. She looked at the clock and winced. She was running late. She thrust her clothes in a bag with her mind on the time ticking mentally creating a checklist.

Make my bed.

Put on my shoes and socks.

Don't forget my journal.

She opened the front door to let in some fresh air. It was still early and the sun was slowly making its debut. She stood at the screen door and let the cool breeze dance across her still moist skin.

Sandra had to connect with Serafine too. Serafine gave her one of the best cabins near the retreat center side. She had a direct view of the lake, and she was minutes from the fellowship hall, Grammy's Kitchen and the center. She eyed a hammock near the lake and added it to her checklist too.

In a whirlwind, she moved around the room like the Tasmanian Devil from Looney Tunes. She tossed her night clothes in the dresser, made her bed with military precision in less than ten minutes Sandra stood back and surveyed her handy work.

She found her shoulder bag and transferred her wallet, some cash, pens, and highlighter from her purse. Last to go in was her journal.

She took a moment to rub her hands over the dated journal. It was old, and it looked it. She had many dreams and plans laid out in it. It was her companion, and it kept her secrets safe. She had entries from as far back as high school. Then she remembered it. The entry lingering over her life like a ball-and-chain.

Sandra flipped it open and skimmed the pages.

"You still have that old thing," Serafine said startling Sandra.

Sandra met her eyes though the screen and slammed the journal close. She dropped it in her bag.

"Hey, you! Good morning."

"Good morning to you too. I knew you wouldn't sleep in. And you've dressed already."

Sandra walked over and opened the screen door. Serafine walked in. The two embraced.

"How'd you sleep?"

"Like a baby."

Serafine sat at the desk, Sandra noticed it was 5:17 sat on the edge of the bed.

"You have plenty of time."

Sandra blushed.

"Early registration starts at 7. The ladies will need time to get in and settled. We will also have a light breakfast setup around 9. The first session begins at 10 in Miriam's Song."

Sandra noticed Serafine's eyes on her watch.

"Miriam's Song is an unusual room name." She

thought it best to move on because her watch was staying.

"I get that a lot," she said with a lighthearted laugh. "I named the rooms after female prophets in the Bible. I will give you a quick tour if you like."

Sandra visited the ranch many times to use the cabins on long weekends. But this would be her first retreat experience.

"I would like that. I am going to make my final call, then I'll be all yours."

"You've decided to join us?" Serafine relaxed with her arm on the back of the chair.

" I think so. However, you must let me still help you out. That's why I came in the first place."

Serafine nodded.

"What should I expect?" Sandra asked pulling her legs beneath her.

"Great question. As my assistant, very little. I will call on you as needed. Helping people find their cabins. Passing out materials here and there. But mostly do what you do best. Love on people." Serafine turned and continued, "I have seen you in your element at the cafe. This is much like that. You are a natural at anticipating people's needs and their tendencies to retreat, no pun intended." She chuckled at her joke. "Here holding back keeps them from experiencing the fullness of the weekend. So I look for loners, ladies having a hard time with concepts, women who look lost."

Sandra knew exactly what Serafine meant since she saw it often with her customers.

"As a retreater," Serafine said, "you have to be

vulnerable. You have to follow me knowing I have your best interest at heart. I am here to assist, but we must let God take the lead."

The thought of letting God take the lead was one she had not considered. She rubbed her hands along her leggings. They were getting sweaty again.

"But Sandra I must warn you, as a retreater I will push and pull at you. I will not give you a pass because you are my friend and sister," she said with a smile. "I will expect you to be all in."

Sandra noticed the mug on the nightstand and reached for it. She took it to the sink and rinsed it out. Was she willing to be open with strangers? She trusted Serafine but she did not know the others.

Serafine sat silent watching her every move. Sandra sat back on the bed.

"With that said I'd love to have you. But you must give as much as you receive. These women have traveled from across the country to have this time and space with God. And as a member of my staff this weekend, we will honor their sacrifice. Understood?"

Sandra understood. Sort of. This was a new Serafine. She liked seeing her friend be direct and expressing her concern. Sandra knew she would do the same for her cafe patrons. Nothing but the best. They gave their hard-earned money and in return she gave them more than coffee. She gave love in every cup.

They both had come a long way.

"So are you still wanting to participate?" Serafine's question cut into her thoughts.

"Yes, I want to help you and participate."

"Good. I'm happy to have you. So now to the housekeeping..."

SANDRA HAD a few hours to report to the check-in. They talked for a while longer before Sandra was given the retreater's packet. She left her to complete the application, questionnaire and release form. The other retreaters did most of their paperwork during the registration process.

Sandra reached for her cellphone and went to her favorites as she walked to the kitchenette. She started another pot of coffee and took the paperwork to the desk.

She recalled Serafine's parting words, "Sandi, don't hold back. You've made the decision now lean into it."

Lean into what? She thought. She shrugged and plopped down into the chair.

Sandra sipped her coffee and made her way through the paperwork. She didn't complete all of it because some of it was beyond her understanding. She would ask Serafine later. Now she had to send her final text.

It was an easy decision. Sandra reached for her phone.

Hey, Knucklehead! I've decided to drink the Kool-Aide.

She smiled from ear to ear as she typed the text
message to Bruce.

She waited for his response and washed her mug.
The whistle from her phone signaled a new message.
She placed it on the drying rack and dried her hands.

Good morning to you too Sunshine! What Kool-Aide?

I'm going to participate in the retreat.

I'm proud of you.

She paused at his response.

Really? Why?

Serafine ain't no joke! I think she'll help you get clarity.

I'm not certain. For right now, I have to turn off my phone. You are my last lifeline.

Sandra laughed.

For you anything. :)

I'm a lucky girl! ;)

Luck has nothing to do with it. But I got you. Text me when you come up for air. Enjoy yourself.

Will do!

Bruce texted the heart emoji. She responded with the smiley emoji with the heart eyes.

"That boy is crazy," she said as she held the power button on her cellphone.

Sandra tossed her phone into her purse and heard a knock on the screen door.

"I'm just checking on you. You ready?"

"As ready as I'm going to be," Sandra passed her packet to Serafine.

"You sure...no turning back," her smile was warm.

Sandra knew she was doing the right thing. But barked, "You make it sound like a life sentence!"

"No, but newbies always remember the first few days vividly. It can be a life-changing experience if you let it."

Sandra will nod. "How about we pray before the ladies show up?" Serafine asked reaching for her hands.

"I'd like that."

Sandra smiled at the warmth of Serafine's hands and closed her eyes as instructed while bowing her head.

Father, thank you. Your grace and love are infinite and too deep and too wide to comprehend. But we thank you.

We are grateful that you loved us first. Grateful for You clearing time for us to come together as sisters, as two seeking you and your perfect will for our lives.

As we enter this day, help us to see You in all things. Help us to see where You are calling us to walk closer to You. Help us to walk away from anything displeasing to You and that is ultimately not for our good. Help us to see where we have strayed and please Father pull us closer to You.

It is You we seek. And although Your ways are beyond our understanding we hope to see Your glory in this. Because our hope is in You.

We bless Your holy name. We submit our pray fully expecting Your absolute best for our lives. We love You.

It's in Jesus' name we pray...

"Amen," Sandra said, wiping the tears from her cheek.

"Amen," Serafine said reaching for Sandra and giving her a strong hug.

The sound of a vehicle crunching across the gravel filled the space between them.

"Ready?" Serafine asks.

"As ready as I'll ever be," she responded with more confidence than she felt.

"Let's get'em, kid."

Sandra laughed, easing her anxious heart.

"After coffee…"

ANTICIPATION

*S*andra crossed the threshold of the Josephine Center. She saw the space with new eyes. There were fourteen women, she recalled from assisting Serafine with check-in. She greeted each of them and gave them gift baskets made by Priscilla. The room now held couches, rockers, and in the back of the room, she noticed a rack with yoga mats, pillows, and a table with refreshments.

The infuser in the corner pumped the room with a soothing scent of citrus and eucalyptus. There was soft music, and Sandra could not determine the composer due to the laughter and chattering, the women were comfortable.

"Ladies, start winding down your conversations," Serafine said.

Sandra didn't know what to expect but women lounging on couches in leggings and t-shirts laughing and talking didn't fit her description of what "counseling" meant in her mind. She felt overdressed in her black slacks and a blouse. Her babydoll slippers were cute but not as comfortable as the flip flops and sandals she noticed the others wore.

Sandra knew from talking with Serafine that the retreat was basically a large group counseling session. She expected the couches, but the casually environment made the atmosphere feel more like friends gathering. It felt more inviting.

The lights were turned down, and the drapes were pulled close. Sandra found the itinerary in her bag. The first session was simple enough, prayer and welcome. The schedule was pretty vague.

Sandra scanned the center noticing a free seat in the back of the room. She beelined to it and was stopped short.

"Don't look so nervous," she said placing a gentle hand on her forearm. "I'm Abigail Howard from Austin. But my friends call me Abby."

Sandra took in the woman's ageless eyes, they were a direct contrast to her silver-grey hair in a neat bun. Sandra relaxed the grip she had on her shoulder bag. Miss Abby was right. She smiled, "Yes, ma'am. Sandra from Houston. Nice to meet you. How are you?"

Sandra was surprised again when instead of accepting her handshake she leaned in and gave her a hug.

"Wonderful baby, I'm here. This is the highlight of my year. Is this your first time?"

"Yes, that obvious?" Sandra returned her radiant smile.

They laughed.

"Yes!" Miss Abby's smile caused her eyes to shimmer.

"What about you?"

Sandra felt more like herself she loved talking with people and learning about their lives. It was one of the things that attracted her to the cafe. She met people from around the world. She learned about their similarities, differences, families, careers, heartaches. Coffee and free time revealed much. She pushed the idea of "counseling" out of her mind and instead saw the women as guests in her cafe.

That made her feel more like herself.

Miss Abby smoothly linked their arms and began to tell about her first experience at the Love Never Fails Retreat.

Sandra glanced down at their intertwines arms, her warm brown skin, and Miss Abby's olive; younger and seasoned.

"Is this okay? My husband always warns me about my touchy nature." She flicked her wrist in a whimsical way, non-apologetic and totally tickled. Miss Abby asked, but Sandra didn't see a trace of shame in her eyes. She kept talking as if they'd known each other for years.

Sandra let Miss Abby lead the way. Listening and asking questions. Her eyes met Serafine's across the room. Serafine tossed a wink her way.

The room was pulsating with... She could almost touch it.

"Ladies, start finding a seat. You have less than three minutes."

Sandra needed to make a quick run for refreshments and find a seat.

"Miss Abby I hope to talk more with you later."

They shared a brief hug and Sandra went to get some juice and find a seat. The corner seat of a couch was still free. She decided to go and drop her bag in it.

"Is this seat taken?" Sandra asked the young lady.

"No." She reached for the basket and binder on the middle cushion.

"Oh no, you don't have to move your things. I think we both can fit just fine if you don't mind. I'm Sandra," she extended her hand.

"Hannah."

"Nice to meet you. Would you like something from the back table?"

Sandra noticed her fidgeting. She assumed she was a little nervous too.

"Water, please."

"Sure, I'll grab our drinks, you save our seats," she said with a smile.

Relaxing she scanned the room again. She could tell which ladies were repeaters and the newbies, like herself. Serafine move about the room laughing and talking. She hugged some. Held hands with others.

Sandra loved seeing Serafine in her element.

"Ladies, one minute. Claim your seats then meet me in the circle."

For the first time, Sandra noticed the chairs in the

back of the room. She hastened her pace to get their waters. Then back to her seat.

She heard Hannah's soft, "Thanks."

Sandra placed her water on the floor on the side of the couch making sure to move it out of the walkway.

Women scurried to the back. Then she noticed a slight countdown being whispered. It felt weird. But she looked from side to side in search of Serafine.

Sure enough, she was whispering too. Along with several other ladies. Their eyes dancing with anticipation. Their excitement was contagious. Sandra started counting down too.

30...

29...

28...

The chairs were set up in two-by-two facing each other, in a circle.

Sandra picked a chair with her back to the wall she wanted to see the entire room. It was a good seat.

15...

14...

13...

Sandra smiled at the woman in front of her, and she did the same.

10...

9...

8...

The countdown grew louder. All of the women seemed to get the point as their voices chanted in unison.

5...

4...

3...

She sat with her full attention on Serafine. The countdown caused the room to palpitate. Sandra's heart beat with anticipation. She too was excited. And that's when it hit her. *What she was feeling was...*

2...

1...

...love.

～

"WELCOME to the Love Never Fails Retreat."

A robust sound of clapping, whistling and talking filled the room each with their eyes on Serafine.

"And this is your inner circle," Serafine made a circling motion with her hand, "in front of you is your sister."

Sandra looked at the beautiful brunette in front of her and smiled, turning her attention back to Serafine.

"You will ask your sister three questions," they began to chatter again.

"Not yet ladies," they laughed at her authoritative tone. "Y'all ain't playing today," she said with a hand on her hip.

She let the laughter die down, and the silence resumed its position before the women and Serafine.

Sandra realized there was no music. Their anticipation hovered over the room like an invited guest.

"You will ask her, as you look in her eyes. What is

your name? Why are you here? How can I pray for you?"

Serafine paused.

"Ladies, those three questions. No more. No less."

Serafine walked the circle placing her hands on random shoulders. Smiling at others.

"And ladies, be a sister to your sister and listen. Listen for the words you hear and the words you see hidden behind her smile."

She stopped next to Sandra and wrapped an arm around her shoulders. She leaned in and hugged her, resting her cheek on Sandra's head.

Sandra returned the hug. Serafine moved on.

"Let's begin."

Sandra met Lilah, they fell into conversation. It was like pulling teeth, but she hoped to chat with her more over the week. Then she heard "Switch."

Surprised, Lilah stood up and so did she out of instinct. The ladies jumped up changing seats. She followed and found another seat.

The chair shuffling continued for almost 20 minutes. Each shift bringing with it giggles and laughter. Each swap helping Sandra to relax more and get to know the women she would serve for the week.

"Now, there are no strangers in this room. Right?" Serafine stated.

"Right," the robust exclamation filled the room. They clapped. She noticed Miss Abby and smiled.

"Find your seats."

They all retraced their steps.

Serafine spent the next half hour teaching them

about love. Sandra listened intently as Serafine talked with such intimacy about God's love. How did she miss it?

"Place your materials aside and get comfortable. You can sit in your seat or the floor. There are mats in the back. You want to sit in an upright position. Your spine long. Try to pull your stomach in to meet your back."

"Girl please..." someone said from the front. The ladies laughed.

"Well, for those of you who can," Serafine stated with a soft smile. They laughed again.

Serafine continued, "Relax your body. Take a deep breath. Close your eyes."

Sandra followed her instructions. She could not recall the last time she sat still and just breathed. Her long days had left her racing. Running from task to task all in the hopes of getting it done.

"Take another deep breath, inhale through your nose, exhale through your nose."

Sandra embraced the release of tension from her shoulders. She opened her eyes for a moment to glance at her watch. She couldn't believe it had been nearly an hour. She glanced up to see Serafine walking between the couches and rockers. She touched shoulders, gave hugs and worked the room.

Their eyes met and Sandra tried to snap her eyes closed. She was caught.

"Close your eye missy, and give me that watch." Serafine whispered in her ear. Sandra did not complain, she gladly handed it over. Sandra was having fun but constantly aware of the time.

Serafine pocketed the watch and continue moving around the room.

"Sisters," Serafine said. The declaration caused Sandra eyes to open again. And she was not alone.

Serafine continued, "Each of you came here for a release. God in His Sovereignty move appointments, personal agendas, deadlines, spouses and everything that could have jeopardized this moment. This moment when your soul needed a change. This moment when your heart felt faint. This moment to give you an opportunity to see Him more clearly. In His Omnipotence He moved it. He pushed it. He erased it. And now you are here. And you my sisters, have a choice to make.," Serafine paused making eye contact with every women in the small room. Each woman looked to have shifted to the end of her seat waiting, like Sandra for Serafine to continue.

"Will you take what He has so graciously offered you? Will you answer the tough questions? Will you be honest with yourself and with the women in this room?" Serafine's arms extended wide as if expanding to the distance of the room.

Would she? Sandra thought to herself. What could she really change in a week? Sitting and talking was all fine and dandy but how would that fix her life? Unless Serafine had Iylana hiding in one of the cabins. And Sandra didn't believe half of the stuff that woman did.

Her life was not an act nor a play. It was complicated, real and messy. And unfortunately she did not get many breaks, so the way Sandra figured, it had to work. *It had to.*

Sandra rubbed her wrist, missing her watch. Miss Abby leaned over from the rocker and whispered, "You'll be just fine dear. After The Release, you'll forget she even has it."

"BREATHE," Serafine stated as she walked the room. "Inhale through your nose, exhale through your nose."

Sandra could not recall the last time she took a deep breath without having her mind laced with the worries of her day. Worries about florist and cake. Worries about coffee beans and salaries.

"Keep breathing ladies. Most live their lives at the whim of others. Your kids and your spouse. Your parents. Your boss. Your employees. I challenge you to breathe.

"Inhale through your nose, let your chest rise, slow and steady." Serafine squeezed Sandra's shoulder.

Sandra looked up at her and smiled.

"Relax. Shoulders down. Neck extended. Belly button touching your spin."

"Still ain't happening baby," Miss Abby said, and a ripple of giggles filled the room.

The room returned to silence. Sandra noticed the music again intertwined with the sound of the women breathing. It was initially erratic, but after a few minutes, all of the women seemed to breathe in unison.

Inhale.

Exhale.

Inhale.

Exhale.

"Get comfortable. Now would be the time to change your seat if needed. There are pillows in the back. We also have yoga mats. There is space along the back wall if you want to sit with support. There is also space up front if you want to layback on a yoga pillow."

Sandra sat her head back and let the slight rock soothe her restless soul. She watched the women scurry and get settled. She tried to remember when she became so restless. And it hit her, like rush and she knew it was when she began entertaining the thought of selling her business.

Sandra felt her chest tighten.

Serafine's voice commanded her presence, "Close your eyes. Inhale. Exhale."

Sandra followed her directive. The tension relieved from her unknowingly holding her breath.

"Inhale...the warm smile you received from someone in this room. Exhale...the first problem that popped into your mind when I told you to close your eyes."

Another wave of light laughed filled the room. Serafine was good.

Sandra decided to set aside the decision of whether she should sell her cafe. She would enjoy all Serafine offered at the retreat in hopes of revisiting it later with a clear mind and heart.

"Inhale...the love and laughter shared during our speed session. Exhale...any negativity that may keep you from experiencing the best God has for you this week."

Serafine continued, "Inhale...God's unfailing love,

His love that called to you before you knew what it was...that held you when you wanted to run...that kept you when you thought you would shatter. Exhale...having to know it all...having to control it all...having to figured it all out."

The soft sounds of sniffles synchronized with the unified breathing.

The women inhaled and exhaled.

Sandra found her mind floating. Empty. Clear.

"Continue to breathe and focus on my voice. Thoughts will leap forward, exhale them out. Inhale God's ability to carry that load for you this week. Let Him," Serafine emphasized.

Sandra rocked. Arms resting on her legs. Chest rising and falling with ease. She let the sounds of the room fade, all that was left was the sound of Serafine's voice.

"The Apostle Paul wrote in Ephesians 3:15-21,"

> *When I think of all this, I fall to my knees and*
> *pray to the Father, the Creator of*
> *everything in heaven and on earth.*
> *I pray that from his glorious, unlimited*
> *resources he will empower you with inner*
> *strength through his Spirit. Then Christ*
> *will make his home in your hearts as you*
> *trust in him. Your roots will grow down*
> *into God's love and keep you strong.*
> *And may you have the power to understand,*
> *as all God's people should, how wide, how*
> *long, how high, and how deep his love is.*

May you experience the love of Christ...

Serafine paused.

> *...though it is too great to understand fully.*
> > *Then you will be made complete with all*
> > *the fullness of life and power that comes*
> > *from God.*
>
> *Now all glory to God, who is able, through his*
> > *mighty power at work within us to*
> > *accomplish infinitely more than we might*
> > *ask or think.*
>
> *Glory to him in the church and in Christ Jesus*
> > *through all generations forever and ever!*
> *Amen.*

A chorus of "Amens" filled the room.

"Inhale... Exhale...

"You made a decision when you got in your car. When you boarded that plane. When you turned onto Jojo's Journey.

"You decided, 'Lord I want more of you' because my heart is too heavy, my life is too complicated, my actions lack love, my doubts are running amok, and my tears have gone from a stream to an ocean. You soul screamed, 'I am tired!'" Her voice bore the ache throbbing within Sandra.

"In response, He says 'Thank you. At your weakest point is where I show My strength. At the end of you is where I do My best work.'"

Sandra's eyes were full of tears, and the constant

flow made it hard to keep her eyes closed. But she would not move. Everything about her was tuned into the moment.

"You decided," Serafine whispered, "and you must decide again, and again, and again...I trust you Lord...I trust you Lord...I trust you Lord."

Sandra repeated the words in her heart. She was tired and she felt broken. And what made it worse was it was all behind closed doors.

Sandra felt the cadence of her breathing increase. And then a squeeze on her shoulder. She inhaled deeply through her nose and exhaled.

"Sisters before you open your eyes, I implore you to decide again. Decide that you will take this week as a gift. Decide to trust His sovereignty, this means He knows the problem, He knows the solution, and by trusting Him, He will connect the dots in your life.

"Decide to entrust God with your doubts, with your difficulties, with the care of your heart. Because the bible tells us His ways are not like our ways. Therefore you must decide to place it in His very capable hands and release your grip on it. What do you decide?" Serafine implored.

Silence lingered like a very attentive participant in the experience. Sandra let the words coax her and the unresolved heartaches of her life.

Sandra decided she would trust Him. She did not fully know what it meant but she knew she tried on her own and it didn't work. She was at the end of herself.

"My sisters," Serafine resumed, "we will slowly open our eyes as we countdown again. From ten to one. And at the end I want you to let is all go and yell at the top of your lungs...release."

Sandra sat up straighter in the rocker.

Serafine started them off "10..."

"9...8...7..."

The chorus of their voices was strong.

"6...5...4..."

Sandra scanned the room. Some ladies stood, others sat, but all of the faces shone with happiness, eyes twinkling with what she would guess was nothing but anticipation for the week to come.

"3...2...1!"

Filled with the squeals of joy and a boisterous burst of applause.

"Release!"

STRONG ROOTS

*S*andra stood on the porch leaning against the beam with her face turned towards the sun absorbing its warmth. She didn't realize it was so cold in the room. But she felt lighter. It was like the first session lifted a ton from her shoulders.

"I'd love to hear more about your cafe during lunch."

Sandra opened her eyes and saw Miss Abby standing beside her. "Sure," she answered with a smile. "Where are you heading now? We have about..." she looked at her wrist for the time and was met with bare skin.

They laughed.

"They ring the bell to give us notice about sessions and meals. You'll be okay without it." Miss Abby said with a wink.

"I guess we'll find out." She rubbed her wrist and pulled her bag up higher on her shoulder.

"I'm heading over to the prayer path I want to walk

it for a while. I'll see you at lunch." Miss Abby stepped down from the porch and headed off.

Sandra wanted to change into something more comfortable and find a place to journal. She walked the short distance to her cabin enjoying the crunching gravel beneath her feet, she waved at Lilah and Alexa heading in the opposite direction.

The morning session was fantastic. Sandra had no idea Serafine was so good. She expected nothing less but in less than two hours she got to know the other ladies and her topic of "God's Love" gave her a lot to journal about.

Sandra entered her cabin and tossed her bag on the bed. She went to the dresser and removed some leggings, and her favorite graphic tee, the large mug on the front said "Got coffee?" it amused her because she always had coffee.

Moments later she exited the bathroom refreshed and with a destination in mind. She would write by the lake. She wanted to stay close so she could hear the bell for lunch because her breakfast of coffee and coffee wasn't smart. She searched her purse for a snack bar, gum or something. She would probably need to get some fruit from Grammy's Kitchen. Then to the lake.

Journaling had always been apart of Sandra's life. At her mom's suggestion, she started writing her thoughts and feelings. Her journals were where she processed her life. But she found it hard to write for the past year. She had many journals but for the retreat she brought her Dreams and Goals journal. It was tattered and old. She had dreams that dated back to high school.

The dream that lingered in her heart. The one that seemed the most illusive and the most difficult to achieve. It was what Sandra thought would make her life complete. It was hidden in the pages, written in ink. So close, yet so far.

Sandra heard a light knock on the screen. She walked over to release the latch.

"Hey," Serafine said. She dug around in her canvas bag and pulled out a handkerchief. She folded in gently into Sandra's hand.

She did not realize she was crying. There was something about witnessing her greatest desire crumble.

"Hey, YOU!" she said drying her face, "Who uses these? I can't remember the last time I saw, let alone used, a handkerchief."

They laughed as they sat at the little table.

"Girl please, you know Grammy had it no other way. That one is actually hand embroidered by her."

Sandra opened it and saw JGL with little purple and pink flowers connected by a vine. They both talked for a while about their grandmothers.

Sandra and Serafine met as kids because their grandmothers lived on the same street. And over school holidays, summer break and church events they became friends, which blossomed to sisters.

"I will treat it with care and return it once I wash it," Sandra said folding it in her hands. "This morning was indescribable."

"I take that as a compliment. I knew you would like it," Serafine said.

"I did. I always knew what you did, but I guess I don't know as much as I thought. I would love to learn more about what you do out here besides this retreat."

"I'd like that too. We can talk shop after this week, but for now, are you ready?" Serafine stood, and Sandra did too.

"For what?" Sandra grabbed her bag and noticed her journal on the bed. She picked it up.

"Your one-on-one?" Serafine said with a smile tugging at the corners of her mouth.

"Uh...sure. I think." Sandra forgot about the one-on-one but remembered seeing it in the retreat packet. She also eyed the folder in Serafine's bag.

"It's harmless."

"Uh huh...I bet. Lead the way," Sandra said closing her cabin door uncertain of what she'd got herself into.

SANDRA FOLLOWED Serafine down the gravel path, the lake in the direct line of their route. She pointed out the other cabins and an area of land she hoped to develop next on the other side of the lake.

They walked in silence for a while and Sandra let her thoughts calm. She felt refreshed after the first session. But she wondered what was next for her. Her plans always fueled her existence. But what if she didn't allow them to dictate her next steps. What would she do next?

"What do you think?" Serafine said pulling Sandra from her thoughts.

Sandra missed them turning. The lake was at their back and a hillside vineyard was before them.

"A vineyard?" Sandra stood with her hand on her hip and used her right hand to shield her eyes from the bright sun.

Serafine smiled and nodded, "A test vineyard."

They stood on the hill overlooking the open land. There were rows of vines stretched on a wire. Sandra wondered how long they had walked. She looked over her shoulder, it must have been a while.

"Do you have grapes?"

"Not yet. But you asked about what I'm working on, and I thought you'd enjoy seeing this. I have a few ideas up my sleeves." Serafine smiled with pure joy on her face.

Sandra knew about plans and how plans changed. But she was happy for her friend.

"What made you decide to start a vineyard? And how long has this been in the works?"

"I'll get into the details later. I thought I'd pique your interest first." She tossed a wink Sandra's way and headed back up the path back towards the lake.

Sandra gave the vineyard one last look. She wondered if Serafine owned the land behind it too. How much land did Miss Josephine leave her? A sista with a vineyard? Impressed Sandra smiled, that would be a sight to behold.

Go 'head girl, she thought as she retraced her steps to catch up with Serafine.

≈

SERAFINE STOPPED at a set of rocking chairs beneath a large tree. The trunk was thick and the span of the branches were massive. Sandra looked up at the tree and the shade it provided. The rocking chairs caught her interest, dropping her bag in the one close by.

"Before you sit, what do you notice about this tree?"

Sandra considered her question. She walked to the tree and touched its rough exterior. She could only imagine how old the tree was and the seasons it had endured. Placed perfectly by the lake. It had a great view, she thought.

"I have no idea. But it has one of the best views on the property."

"I'd have to agree," Serafine laughed, and met Sandra's eyes. "Deborah is about 400 years old. It has been here a long time. Can you imagine the lives that have come and gone on this land? The hardships, the victories...," she looked up and so did Sandra, "the declarations of love under the shade of its expansive branches, the tears the roots have absorbed."

Sandra could imagine a picnic basket and cloth spread with lovers whispering their declarations of love. *Would it ever be for her?* Probably not. She didn't have that with Alonso, and she knew it. And she knew he did too.

"Beneath your feet are roots that are more expansive that what you see before you. Roots that ensured its survival." Serafine was next to the tree, her facial features danced in awe of the tree's existence. Her hands flat on the tree gliding across its rough service.

"Roots are the lifeline. This tree is no different from

us. Weathering the sessions of life. From season to season, life gives rain, the sun provides warmth and harsh seasons threaten to break the very branches that give the ability to expand and shade the foundation holding it all together."

Sandra listened and consider the roots beneath her feet. She joined her bag in the rocker and laid her head back as Serafine continued. What about her roots?

Sandra had her parents and grandparents. Then there was her sister, Cindy—she loved that crazy girl. Sandra smiled at the thought of her baby sister being a mother, and she would be an aunt. They had all weathered life together, and they stood strong.

The thoughts of her family made her heart happy. She knew it was a trying season, but the James' always managed to emerge stronger than ever.

Sandra counted Serafine as part of her roots and her girls Alicia, Faith, and Danyelle too.

And Bruce, Sandra couldn't forget him. He made her life complete.

Where did that thought come from?

The two were friends, best friends, and there was nothing in life that she couldn't share with him. But her relationship with Alonso had caused distance in their friendship, and she vowed to would change that when she returned home. Bruce was worth it.

Serafine had joined her in the other weathered rocking chair. She pulled a folder out of her bag and a blue pen. She leaned on the arm and twisted her body to face Sandra.

Sandra glanced at the label on the folder with her

name. She noticed notes scribbled in Serafine's delicate cursive handwriting with loops and swirls here and there.

"As stated in the packet, everything is confidential, and these help me serve you better," Serafine gestured to the file open on her lap.

Sandra nodded. She wasn't sure where to begin or her feelings about having a formal counseling session with her friend. But she trusted Serafine yet she never felt counseling was a necessity, her mother taught her to shake it off.

You don't like something, shake it off. Someone hurts your feelings, shake it off. But for some reason she couldn't shake this off.

"Let's start with why are you here, I have seen more tears from you in the past day than I have our entire lives. Well, except for the time Grammy got us with her switch for eating all of her tomatoes."

They laughed until they cried, happy tears.

They were about seven years old and stuck outside. Their grandmothers had a rule, once outside you stayed outside until you wanted to return inside.

They would drink from the water hose and play. But one day they got hungry and didn't want to cut their time short. Serafine suggested the plump tomatoes in Miss Josephine's garden.

The two quietly plucked the tomatoes from the garden gathering them in their shirts. It was hard to walk without squashing them. As giggled tiptoeing past the window, they went to the park and found a tree much like Deborah. They sat and ate the sweet red tomatoes, talking and laughing about their futures away from grandmothers, rules, and boys.

Little did they know that their day would end with being grounded for eternity.

"Those tomatoes were good," Sandra proclaimed.

"Yes, they were. Grammy reminded me of that day every time I visited." She recalled with a smile.

Serafine kept a close eye on Sandra, making Sandra feel exposed. Serafine knew her like very few people. She decided to trust God and Serafine with her secrets, in hopes she would lighten her burdens even more.

Sandra rocked and closed her eyes. She had to dig into the corners of her mind and dust off her reason. Initially, she thought it was to get away from her sister and the wedding. She wanted to reflect without the demands of life hanging over her head. But that morning after session she decided, she would be honest with herself. Maybe that's what Serafine meant by leaning into the experience.

"A few months ago, I started having panic attacks." She stopped rocking and turned her face heavenward as a gentle breeze danced across her face. The leaves on Deborah danced, and the branches swayed. She saw Serafine freeze with pen in her left hand, hovering over the page.

"Tell me about it," Serafine said.

"Life," Sandra shrugged it off.

"What was going on when you had the first one?" Serafine asked.

What had she been doing? Sandra thought. Then she remembered, "I was at home one evening. I believed I was having a heart attack. My chest was tight, my breathing was short, and my heart raced. It was the scariest experience of my life."

Serafine reached for her hand resting on the arm of the rocker. "Then what happened?"

"I freaked out and called 911 and hung up. They called right back and asked a bunch of questions. Eventually, I drove myself to the hospital, and the doctors found nothing wrong with me."

Serafine scribbled in the folder. "What were you doing just before it happened?"

Sandra thought back. "I was reviewing a few bids."

"Bids?" Her eyebrows arched.

"Yes, for my cafe." Sandra knew this piece of information would be new to Serafine but she had a feeling it was part of her panic attacks. She never did well with change.

"Bids for what?"

"I am thinking of selling my cafe. I'm ready for something different." She exhaled. It felt good getting that off her chest. Serafine was the first to know besides the potential buyers.

"Different? Like what, you want to move, new business?"

Sandra shrugged, "At this point all of it." She looked over the water. She wondered if it was as cool as it appeared. Then she touched her hair. She had fresh twists. She'd have to take a swim next time.

"Why did the thought of selling cause you so much anxiousness?"

Sandra opened her eyes and leaned forward resting

her arms on her knees. "I'm not sure. I think it was a cross between it being a new chapter and my life not being exactly how I'd planned."

"What had you planned?"

Sandra grabbed her bag from the back of the rocker. She dug around and pulled out her Dream Journal. She caressed it and whispered, "I wanted it all. Husband, kids, and my business."

"Is that what you want?" Serafine asked.

"No, I don't think its realistic...or even possible."

"Really? Why is that?" Serafine asked, writing again in the folder.

Sandra explained the state of her relationship with Alonso and how her business was growing, but it required more of her time and the strain it caused on her relationships. "And I'm 37!"

"And?" Serafine retorted. "Now, don't you act like we are old as dirt. I'm the same age as you."

They laughed.

"But look at what you've done in your 37 years." Sandra used her hand to gesture to the property, "And the lives you are changing." She squeezed Serafine's hand and said, "I'm so proud of you and Miss Josephine would be too."

"Thank you," Serafine said with tears in her eyes.

It had been more than 10 years since Miss Josephine's death. Serafine had done an exceptional job with the center and turning her life around.

"Did another panic attack bring on this trip?"

"No, I wanted to help you. Honestly, it was a reason to run."

"Run from what? Or whom?" Serafine pulled a handkerchief from her bag and wiped her eyes and nose.

"Both."

Sandra explained the wedding, the babies and her struggle with whether to sell and how it would change her life.

"Congrats," Serafine said. "What is it that you want now? And before you answer, there is no right or wrong answer."

Sandra used the technique from the morning session. She inhaled deeply through her nose and exhaled. She let her hands run over the worn fabric of her old journal.

She responded, barely above a whisper, "I want a husband, kids, dog...okay maybe not the dog." She laughed, she liked dogs but the thought of dog hair on her furniture was enough to scratch that part of her dream. "I want it all. But what I wanted most is love."

Sandra felt a bit lighter. Talking was helping. It wasn't changing anything but getting it out made it feel doable. Maybe.

"So what is your prayer?" Serafine asked.

"To gracefully release this desire. To let it go and not be angry about releasing it as I watch my sister get it all." Her response rolled out so fast she did not filter what she was saying. *She was angry.* But she loved her sister. "I'm the worse sister ever!"

"No dear, you're not. You're human. That's all. No more. No less," Serafine declared.

The bell chimed in the distance.

Sandra felt awful. How could she have these feeling about her sister? She looked in the distance as the women started walked to Grammy's Kitchen.

"If there is another way to address your feeling and thoughts, would you be willing to consider it? We cannot address all of your concerns this week, but I think together we can make progress." Serafine said.

"Really?"

Serafine nodded.

"I love my sister, Serafine, I do."

"I know. And I know this has nothing to do with your sister and everything to do with you."

The intense expression on Serafine's face caused Sandra to pause. "What do you mean?"

"Let's head to lunch now. I will explain over the next day or so. But I will leave you to think about two things: Do you trust God and are you willing to do the work?"

Without hesitation, Sandra responded, "I do, and I am."

"*H*onestly, I'd do just about anything to get my peace back," Sandra said more to herself than Serafine.

"I understand the feeling. But know that it didn't happen overnight, and it won't change overnight." She stood and placed the folder and pen in her bag. Serafine stopped and turned to Sandra.

Sandra knew it wouldn't all just go away. Boy, wouldn't that be wonderful, she thought. She confessed, "I'm not afraid of hard work. However, this touchy-feely stuff makes me uncomfortable."

Serafine laughed, "I'm sure."

They started walking to Grammy's for lunch.

"When did you get so..." she searched for the right words, not wanting to offend Serafine, "religious." She said using her fingers to make the quotation marks.

"I'm not religious, per se," she too emphasized the word with air quotation marks. "I've just learned a lot about life. The good and bad. The highs and lows. And you want to know the truth..."

Sandra turned to face her, and they stopped again. Miss Abby walked pass and said, "I'll save you a seat, Sandra."

"Thanks!" She said to her back, giving Serafine her full attention again. "I'm listening..."

"Our grandmothers were always right. Grammy had a direct line to Jesus. That woman could pray you from the top of your head to the soles of your shoes and then act a fool over her tomatoes."

"Miss Josephine was a mess!"

"You ain't told me nothin'!" Serafine folded over laughing. "For real," Serafine said wiping the tears from her eyes, "It all begins and ends with Jesus. I mean, I always believed them, but I didn't trust it, you know."

Sandra nodded.

"Life had a way of making their Jesus talk sound like just that, talk. Like it didn't hold up against gadgets and self-help books. Like they just didn't know any better."

Sandra only wished she'd listened more. She may have saved herself a lot of heartache and trials.

Serafine continue, "How much have you read your bible?"

"I plead the Fifth," she held up her hand like she was being sworn in, "I will not incriminate myself."

"What am I going to do with you? I will address this differently, so you don't have to incriminate your crazy behind," Serafine shook her head in amusement. "My training is in biblical counseling. This means I counsel using scripture believing it is the source for all of our answers."

Serafine went on to explain it more as they walked. Sandra was curious, it was the first time she heard the term. But she was game.

She could smell the food, and her stomach growled. Sandra smiled.

"Let me give your first assignment," smiling back. "Scripture tells us that we are to operate in godly wisdom. The Bible is how we gain that wisdom along with the Holy Spirit. For now, know that any unloving attitudes you carry in your heart towards anyone will cause an outward response in your life."

"Unloving, what do you mean? I love my sister."

"I know you do. So don't think of it as affection but we have to consider again the love God speaks of in Scripture. For example, the Bible tells us if we are bitter or jealous of another we can expect disorder in our lives. And this is towards anyone, your sister, Alonso, and even God."

"Really? I love God. I'm not a perfect Christian. But I do love Him."

Serafine nodded her head.

Sandra never heard that before. To be honest, she hadn't read her bible outside of church since she was a kid. She may have looked at a passage here and there but she never actually read it for the sake of reading.

"It's not about perfection. And it won't be resolved overnight," Serafine wrapped an arm around Sandra. "I'll be here to help you."

Sandra nodded. How could she not love her sister?

And God? That couldn't be true. Her thoughts were going a mile a minute. She felt her heart begin to race.

"Don't worry. I'm telling you this now because I want you to know there is an answer and you are not alone."

"Thank you." She took several deep breaths. She would not jump to conclusions. She had to trust God. She would start with listening and doing the work. She had to believe it would get better.

"You're a story lover," Serafine stated. "I want you to write a list of all the major characters in your life and share their roles."

Sandra pulled out her notebook and began writing.

Serafine continued, "Write the major ones. Start with those connected with your trip here, and you could also consider those associated with your first panic attack."

Sandra nodded.

"Then list all the gifts and talents you believe you are equipped with to address the pressing issues in your life."

Serafine paused as a few women passed them.

"Once you have it all jotted down, I want you to answer this statement in written form. 'My name is Sandra. Like the oak tree, I'm rooted in.... And because of my roots, I am certain I was created to ....'"

Serafine repeated the statement a few more times as Sandra wrote it in her Dreams Journal. She closed it and slipped it back into her bag.

"Do you believe this is all due to these unloving thoughts?" Sandra asked she had to know.

"Well, on the one hand, it's not that easy but on the

other is may be the root cause of what you're experiencing. Remember Deborah and her deep and wide roots. Just think about what would happen is her roots were rotten. How would that effect her?"

Sandra thought about it, "I'd assume that she wouldn't grow. Not as full and expansive as she is now."

"Right. Roots determine the health of the tree. And your roots determine the health of life and your ability to be fruitful. Unhealthy roots bear rotten fruit." Serafine said with a shrug.

Sandra gazed over her shoulder. *Did she have unhealthy roots?* She thought back to their time beneath the tree and her list. She was determined to find out.

"Let me eat and get to this assignment because I want healthy roots."

SANDRA WAS full and ready to start her assignment. She stepped out of Grammy's Kitchen and walked towards her cabin. Her life was full of characters, she considered her people again. Dad, mom, Cindy, her grandparents, Bruce, Serafine. Her list was growing, but she needed to sit down and write it out. She decided to head back to the rocking chairs beneath Deborah.

Sandra ventured back to the tree and saw Serafine there with another woman. She nodded in their direction and continued her walk along the lake.

Sandra thought talking to Serafine would help her get some clarity, and it had, but it also left her with more questions. All of the talk about trusting God and unloving thoughts still had her confused.

Sandra gave her life to Christ when she was twelve and never gave it a lot of thought. She treated people fairly, and she was a good person. She attended church when she didn't have to work but would all that classify as having a relationship with Christ. Did it mean she trusted God?

Sandra found a grassy patch next to the lake. She pulled out her journal and reviewed the notes from her session with Serafine. She turned the page to a blank sheet. She drew lines across the top, bottom and one vertically down the page. Sandra decided to start her list with God. She left the role blank. He was God. That was a role too. *Right*? She shrugged tossing it back into her bag.

Sander wondered if she'd get a signal strong enough to use her cellphone. She looked around. She wasn't in a heavily treed area. Making a call would break the rules. Serafine would kill her.

She went back to her list. She wrote Jesus and left His role blank too. Next then her parents, she listed them separately. She took a few minutes to add roles alongside their names. They offer much more than their parental guidance in her life.

Bruce. Her pen tapped the page as she considered his role. Sandra looked over her shoulders. She was the only one in sight. She grabbed her cellphone and text Bruce.

Got a second?

Sandra smiled when she noticed the little typing bubble on her screen.

A lifetime for you.

She felt like a teenager sneaking around. She laughed, dialing Bruce.

"What's up rule breaker?" His voice several octaves higher than his usual deep baritone.

"Name calling. Is that what we've come to?" She wrote *my happy place* in her journal beside his name.

"My bad. You alright?" Bruce said calmly, and their comfortable silence calmed her thoughts. She wanted to tell him everything.

"Yes. No. I don't know..."

"Take it from the top."

Sandra wiggled on the grass to cross her legs, thankful she put on leggings. She tossed her journal on top of her bag. Sandra deeply inhaled and exhaled looking over the water, the day was gorgeous. She loved Serafine's ranch.

Bruce held the line and let the silence rest between them. Sandra watched the birds fly across the sky tree hopping. The peace of the environment etched its way into her body. Her shoulders relaxed.

"Thank you."

"For what?"

"Being you. You are one of the few people in my life who is not pushing and pulling me. And I can...," Sandra could *be herself*, "Just thank you."

"You got it. Where's this coming from? I appreciate

your gratitude. But you have me beginning to worry. You don't sound like yourself."

She appreciated his concern, "Do you think women have a mid-life crisis?"

He laughed. His boisterous laugh nudged away the shadows lurking in her heart and chipped at the disappointment threatening to make Sandra feel defeated.

"Did you buy an Aston Martin and run off with a younger dude?"

"Ahhhh, he's got jokes folks!" Her laughter married with his.

Bruce gathered himself and responded, "No, Sandra. I don't believe there is such a thing, but if there is I'm sure gender has nothing to do with it. Why do you ask?"

"Don't laugh again."

"I can't promise. But I'll try."

This man, she thought.

"And stop smiling," Sandra ordered.

"You are absolutely no fun. Stop stalling. Spill it."

$\sim$

SANDRA PULLED A BLADE OF GRASS. Talking to Bruce was like talking to herself. There was an ease that was rare. She started where their last conversation ended.

She followed his command and spilled it. All of it. Cindy. The babies. Serafine's statements about Sandra's unloving thoughts. Sandra's dissatisfaction with her life. How much she loved the ranch and all about Deborah too.

Bruce was Bruce. He listened. He asked questions and knew when to let her process it aloud.

Sandra also shared toying with the idea of selling her cafe, Coffee Confessions.

"Why?" he asked.

"It's not the same," she said brushing her hand over the grass. "The past few years I've felt more and more disconnected. I'm working and working. It once felt like my home away from home. Now...."

"Do you have someone handling it for you? Yes, I'm using my attorney. We've received some great bids. I will walk away from the deal a wealthy woman."

"But is this what you want?"

"No. I'm not sure. But I don't see how I can have what I want most when my life is soldered to the cafe." The thought of not having Coffee Confessions made her cringe. Who would she be without it? It was her baby. But it seemed like she couldn't have it all. Something had to go.

"Let me help. I can come back while you figure it out," Bruce stated in a plea.

"I'm a big girl." She declined.

"Yeah," he sounded unconvinced, "but you're not Superwoman. Sandi, let me help."

"Thank you, but I can do it. Besides, what kind of friend would I be asking you to walk away from your business because I'm overcommitted and burnt out." She shrugged, "My plan is to hold off until after the wedding unless I get an irresistible offer."

"How can you laugh about something so serious? What would you do after selling it?"

Sandra looked across the water at the vacant land Serafine pointed out during their walk. *What if...*

"I don't know. Invest in another company. Start a new business in a small town. I could devote my efforts to...."

"To what?"

She hesitated, she decided to get it off her chest, "I want to start a family. And who says you need a husband to have kids? Women do it alone every day."

"What?" his voice raised, "Now I know something is wrong with you. Have you ran this idea by your father?"

Sandra sat straight up, her back stiff as a board. She was grown. She could do what she wanted. It was her life.

"Sandi, have you?"

"No, just you."

"Just me?"

Sandra could hear the smile his voice, and she smiled along. She rolled her eyes, her mouth puckered with a mock attitude, "Yes Bruce, just you."

VISITOR

"*S*andi..."

Sandra's eyes shot open with a sharp intake of her breath. Serafine stood next to the hammock with her hand on Sandra's shoulder.

"Hey Sleeping Beauty," Serafine smiled, but it did not reach her eyes. Her smile was tight as she waited for Sandra to wake.

Sandra extended her arms to stretch. Her back curved and twisted, causing the hammock to swing a little. Serafine took a short step back.

Sandra was napping beneath Deborah, her absolute favorite spot at Loving Ranch. Over the course of the week, everyone knew where to find her, in that exact spot after group sessions. Sometimes with the other ladies, but most of the time she was alone.

Yes, she loved Serafine's tree, she thought. Cascaded by its protective leaves and welcoming shade she wondered how long she'd been asleep. But since she didn't have a watch she shrugged.

"Did I miss our session?" Sandra asked.

"No."

Sandra couldn't believe it had been five days. She embraced the knowledge Serafine shared during each session. And it helped even more once it dawned on her that she had not experienced an anxiety since arriving at the ranch.

Over the first few days of the retreat, Serafine used each session and exercises to pinpointed the sources of her anxiety—at least some of it. She was sure there was more buried inside her. But at the moment, Sandra was content with taking Serafine's lead.

Sandra learned with Serafine's help that the culprit was her runaway thoughts and her lack of trusting God's sovereignty, which turned out to be the root of many of her unfruitful circumstances. She was not cured, but she felt better. And each day her racing heart had calmed a little more than the day before.

"What's up then? You don't look too happy, and I know it's not me because I'm your best student."

"My best student? Yeah right."

They shared a laugh. Sandra moved to sit up and her journal and pen slide down her chest to the hammock. She rubbed her eyes with the heels of her hands.

"You have a guest." The slow delivery and tightness in her voice caught Sandra's attention.

"A guest? I'm not expecting anyone."

"It's me."

Sandra heard over Serafine's shoulder. She knew the voice. *What was he doing at the ranch?* She thought.

Serafine stepped aside and there stood Alonso.

"Thanks, Serafine," she said not taking her eyes off Alonso.

"Call me if you need me. It was nice seeing you again."

"You too."

Serafine headed back towards the cabins leaving the two alone with only the sound of gravel crunching with Serafine's departure.

Sandra couldn't believe his arrogance of just popping up. That was just like him. He didn't listen. He didn't give her space to breath. He pushed and pulled at Sandra until the topics of marriage, family, and a future arose. Then the brother was faster than Usain Bolt.

"For you, they're not as beautiful as you, but few things are." He gave Sandra a bouquet of roses and kissed her on the cheek.

"I can't believe you drove out here," Sandra said as her nose brushed the soft red petals.

"I didn't. I hired a car service. I got some work done," he shrugged and swatted at a bug dancing around his face.

"You should sit in this very spot in the evening. The sunset is breathtaking," she said hiding a smile in her roses. Alonso was a city boy. Nothing about him enjoyed the outdoors unless it was getting him from the building to the car.

"What you got there?" He said bending to pick up her journal.

"Nothing," Sandra stood snatched it back and tossed it back on the hammock. "I appreciate the flowers, but you have to leave. I need this time. Alone."

"Sandi I'm trying here." He looked frustrated. He rubbed the back of his neck. "Doesn't that count for anything?"

"Why?"

"Why what?"

"Why are you here? You know what I want. And I'm tired of sounding like a broken record." Flowers, cards, trips were easy. Commitment was hard. Sandra was exhausted, and trying to make his square butt fit in a round space within her life proved impossible.

"What's the hurry? Why can't we enjoy each other and let things naturally evolve?"

"I'm not waiting around while you try to figure out whether you want a family or not. Whether you want me or not." She thrust Alonso's flowers in his chest.

"I want you, baby. I'm here to prove that I do. I just don't want marriage. Not right now." He reached for her.

Sandra stepped out of his grasp. She didn't want Alonso near her.

She was sick and tired of the same disagreement. The same lines were drawn in the sand dividing them. Alonso on the side of perpetual dating, Sandra on the side of happily-ever-after in marriage.

She wiped her sweaty hands on shorts. For the first time all week her heart responded negatively to their conversation. It announced its rejection of Alonso's presence as it pulsated rapidly in her chest.

She saw his lips moving but couldn't hear what he was saying. She crossed her hands over her chest taking several deep breaths.

"Just go."

Alonso placed his hands on each arm and pulled her into his embrace.

Sandra let herself have a brief moment of being cradled in his arms. She rested her head on his chest. He smelled fresh but artificial and out of place with his crisp white dress shirt against his warm caramel complexion.

Maybe she was pushing him. Maybe he deserved a chance. Sandra considered giving him time and trusting his professed love for her. She experienced a lot of clarity for herself in less than a week from getting a little space, she considered extending the same grace to him.

Sandra and Alonso stood for several minutes. She was a cuddler, and he knew it. But the definition of insanity was doing the same thing over and over and expecting a different result. She wanted something different. And this...*he was not it*.

Sandra pulled back and smoothed at the invisible wrinkles in his shirt.

"How about this? We can move in together and give it a try." He gathered her hands between his and lifted them to his soft lips.

"Try..." Sandra repeated his words removing her hands from his. "No, Alonso. That just won't do."

"Sandra, what do you want from me? I shower you with gifts. I'm available to you whenever you need. I love you. Why is that not enough?" His arms extended in the arm as if he was being crucified.

"Because I want more..." she whispered crossing her arms over her chest.

They went back and forth neither giving or relenting.

"Baby are you okay? I can hear you two over at the cabins."

Sandra blinked and turned to see Miss Abby.

"I'm sorry. I didn't realize. We're almost done."

"Are you sure?" Miss Abby shot a stern look at Alonso.

"Yes, ma'am."

They stood in a strained silence as Miss Abby retraced her steps.

Sandra turned back to Alonso with her fists clutched at her side. "You have to leave."

"Promise me we'll have dinner when you get back. We can fix this."

"No, Alonso," she shook her head, "there is nothing to fix. We want different things. You want to play house. I want a husband. I think we should cut our ties and part as friends."

"Why do you always have to be in charge? You decide when we see each other. You decide when we have sex. You decide when it's date night. And don't let me buy tickets to a concert or a play and forget to add it to your precious calendar." He waived his hands comically in the air, as if exasperated. "Frankly, I think you should marry yourself. Because you obviously don't have room in your life for a man." His voice swelled with each blow to her soul.

Sandra winced at Alonso's words. *Now it all comes out*, she thought. Normally he was all, "Yes, Sandi." "Sure, Sandi." "Anything for you Sandi." Alonso continued his rant laying the decline of their relationship at her feet, like it was all her fault. Sandra cringed watching his mouth move and his arms thrashing in the air. *She would look like a fool again.*

Sandra's head swam with the accusations she'd have to endure for another failed relationship. Her heart rate increased, and the shade from Deborah provided no reprieve from her increased body temperature. She could feel an attack hanging at the edge of her patience as Alonso continued.

Sandra walked to the tree and rested her back against it.

"What's wrong with you? Why are you sweating? Let me get you to your room." Alonso reached for her again. She stopped him, her hands lifted towards him. He froze.

"I don't need your help," she said between clenched teeth. "What I need you to do is leave." Sandra felt lightheaded. She bent over placing her hands on her knees. Her attempts to take a deep breath failed and stopped short in her throat.

Sandra tilted her head back but could not breathe. She lowered to the grass. She could hear mother, her father, her sister, their friends. Tears filled her eyes.

Alonso didn't want a relationship. He wanted arm

candy. But no more. She didn't need him. She didn't need anyone.

"Go!" She yelled the birds fluttered away from the hostility in her tone.

"What is going on here?" Serafine said stared between from her to him. She walked over to Sandra, crossing in front of Alonso. Serafine placed her palm on Sandra's forehead. "Please leave please," she asked Alonso, "I'll have her call you later."

He paused and assessed Sandra's state and stepped towards her. But Serafine blocked his attempt.

"I will call security. Don't make me do it because I will." Serafine placed her arm around Sandra, not taking her eyes off Alonso.

"I don't want to lose you. I'll make this right," he said to Sandra.

"But you already have." Sandra's tears flowed as she leaned into Serafine for support.

"I'm giving you five minutes to exit my property, or I'll have someone escort you off." Serafine's words cut through the fog in Sandra's head.

Sandra wished she could see his face but the tightness in her chest made it hard to focus on either of them.

"Whatever, I'll leave. But this is not over Sandi."

Sandra watched him walk away in the haze of her pain and her tears.

"Sandi, what is happening?" Serafine kneeled beside her and used the hem of her shirt to dab the side of Sandra's face.

"I can't...can't—"

"Stop, honey. Save your energy. I'm calling 911." She reached into her pocket and pulled out her cellphone.

"No..." Sandra murmured. She felt Serafine slide her arms around her shoulders and pull her close.

Sandra allowed her head to rest. She knew if she could just quiet her thoughts and steady her breathing everything would be all right.

Serafine talked into her phone rubbing small circles on Sandra's back. She couldn't make out the words over the thunderous sound of her heart banging on her sternum.

Sandra's skin felt like a forest fire spread from her head to her feet. She saw the crowd gathering around her and heard their mumbling voices. She was embarrassed but couldn't stop as the panic attack seized control of her body. She couldn't control her life. She couldn't fix her relationship. And the fact that her parents never liked Alonso embarrassed her even more.

Boy, could she pick'em. When would she learn?

"Breathe Sandi, baby. Please. They are almost here."

God please..., she prayed, *help me.*

Then everything went black.

PANIC

*S*andra heard beeping. It wasn't an alarm or a reminder alert. It was a steady...beep, beep, beep. Thoughts of investigating it further flutter through her mind, but she slipped back into a deep sound sleep.

WHAT TIME WAS IT? The backdrop of the beeping persisted. *Was it time to get to the shop?*

Sandra struggled to open her eyes. She forced her eyes to comply, but they fell closed again. Her lids weighed a ton. She lifted her hand to rub her eyes and felt something moving across her body.

"What the he—" Sandra whispered, her voice hoarse. Her eyes shot open, the room was dark, and she noticed the IV in her arm. She wanted to sit up and get out the bed.

Oh no...no, no, it happened again. Sandra tried to turn on her right side but was distracted by the constant beep. She looked over and saw an EKG machine.

Sandra felt a touch on her left arm and jumped. Her eyes swiped through the darkness for the source and her eyes met his.

"You scared me," he whispered.

Her eyes clouded with tears. She turned on her side moving closer to see him better, she laid her right arm along her hip careful of the IV. "Sorry...," she whispered. She reached for him, and he didn't hesitate, he engulfed her hand in his.

He placed a soft kiss on her hand.

"Where.... How...," she couldn't decide what she wanted to know first.

"You are in the hospital. Relax, Sweet Sandi. I got you." Bruce wiped at the tears streaming across her face gathering in a small puddle on the hospital bed. The mattress was soft, but the steel bed bar between made her cringe.

Sandra nodded, relief washed over her. Her eyes grew heavy again.

"Let me go get a nurse. I'll be back." Bruce stood from the chair stretching to his full six foot two inches, not releasing her hand. He rolled his shoulders. He bent over and placed a soft kiss on her forehead.

He hovered near looking in her eyes. He squeezed Sandra's hand once more before releasing it.

"Okay..." Sandra said, immediately missing his warmth. She watched him walk to the door, and a flood of white light entered the dark room. He stepped into the hall pulling the door closed behind him. She adjusted to her back and decided to rest a little while she waited.

She smiled in the cold dark room. *He came...*

Sandra fell asleep again.

∽

"I FEEL LIKE A HUMAN PIN CUSHION," Sandra growled under her breath, shooting the nurse a nasty stare. The constant prodding and repeated attempts to draw blood left bruises on her arms.

"Better safe than sorry. So, stop complaining and let the woman do her job," Bruce smiled with lazy eyes.

Sandra noticed the slight bags under his eyes, he was tired. The worry lingering in his eyes made her heart warm. He stayed by her side for the past two days. He watched over her while she slept, he took the hundreds of calls and not once did he complain. She decided to take his lead and do the same.

"I know that chair is uncomfortable," she said after the nurse left them alone. Bruce stopped fighting with the raggedy foldout bed after the first night and chose to sleep at the foot of her bed using his crossed arms as a pillow. "Why don't you go to the ranch and sleep in a real bed?"

"I'll leave when you leave," he said with finality.

Sandra was too scared to be embarrassed. Her first thoughts were about what Serafine and the women at the retreat must have thought. She never passed out during a panic attack. And that left her scared to death. *What if she'd been home alone? Or worse, driving?*

Bruce was right. She would take every test they advised to determine how she could get better. The ambulance took her to the small local hospital, and the staff remained in contact with her physician in town.

"Miss James," Dr. Charles said tapping on the door with a knuckle.

"Hello Doctor, so what's the verdict?" Sandra sat up and tucked the paper gown under her thighs.

Dr. Charles looked to be in his 60s with bright eyes and a matching smile. "Well, it may seem odd, but you are perfectly healthy."

The confusion must have shown on Sandra's face because he sat on the rolling stool and pulled closer to show her the charts. It all was foreign to her, the terms and numbers scribbled before her eyes didn't help her understand what she'd experienced.

"We ran our usual tests along with a couple recommended by your doctor to be safe. You are a healthy young woman."

"But...but...how do you explain what happened to me? That can't be normal."

"I can see why it would cause you some confusion, and you're right, it's not normal. What type of work do you do?"

"I own a cafe."

He nodded, jotting in the file. He closed it and looked back at her. "On a level between one and ten, one being no stress, ten being extremely stressful, how would you rate your daily stress level?"

Sandra shrugged and made sure not to look over at Bruce. She felt his eyes on her.

"It comes and goes, but for the most part it is pretty routine stuff."

Bruce cleared his throat but didn't say a word.

"Most days," she added. Still not looking his way. Serafine knew her life was nonstop. She had the cafe, employees, Cindy's wedding.

"Miss James, it seems that you had a panic attack. It is rare for someone to faint or black out, but based on what you've told me that is what you experienced." Dr. Charles paused, she assumed he was letting his words sink in.

"You are saying your job isn't stressful, but something caused your body to physically react to the point of shutting down. According to your test, you are fine, but that nasty bump on your head says differently."

Sandra's hand grazed the patch on the back of her head. Serafine was with her but apparently when she blacked out her head fell back against the tree. The staff called the ambulance and Alonso had to be escorted from the property.

Sandra didn't remember much except waking up in the hospital and finding Bruce by her side.

Bruce stood and walked to the bed. He sat and pulled her close to him. "Don't cry, baby. Please don't cry." He whispered in her ear.

Sandra nodded and buried her face in his neck.

"So what do you recommend Dr. Charles," Bruce asked. She could feel the rhythm of his heart. She was safe with him.

"Rest," he responded. "She needs to pinpoint what the source is. Because she is fortunate that she was sitting. She could have been driving or walking or somewhere alone. Now, if she experiences it again, I'd recommend having her doctor run more tests. But like I said," he shrugged, "we don't see anything that would cause us to be alarmed or concerned. Other than us knowing that something caused her to pass out."

"Yes, sir."

"Due to the circumstances, I am advising her to stay one more night. We'll watch her, and if all is well, I'll release her in the morning. But only if someone will escort her home. She is ordered not to drive until she receives clearance from her regular physician."

"I'll take her home," Bruce confirmed.

They talked for a while longer. Sandra heard them but couldn't believe she let herself get to that point. She was in the hospital. *The hospital.*

She ran to Loving Ranch to relax only to experience another panic attack. It was not getting better but worse.

Dr. Charles left them alone saying he would return in the morning.

"Serafine was right," she whispered still encircled in Bruce's arms.

SANDRA TOLD Bruce about the retreat and her private sessions with Serafine.

"She helped me see that I didn't trust God," she explained, "and how my attacks are due to some unresolved matters in my relationship with Him."

Bruce listened. Asking questions here and there.

Sandra continued, "And she is right."

"Right about what exactly," he asked.

"I don't know...I guess that somewhere I got it in my mind that I could fix the ailments in my life."

Sandra let the sound of that statement settle over them. She knew that was the issue. But Sandra was a go-getter and driven. However, somewhere along the way, she became her own god. The captain of her own life, slowly edging God out. *And look at the mess I'm in because of it*, she thought.

"What are these ailments that you're trying to self-correct?"

"Everything. Selling the shop, my relationship with Alonso, my sister's wedding, my weight, my health, will I ever experience real love." Her heart fluttered with anxiety.

Sandra mentally ran through the laundry list of all the things she had to release to God. All the things she held with an iron grip. *But could she?* Her heart filled with emotion.

Sandra dug her face deeper into the warmth that Bruce offered without strings, without expectations, without questions.

Sandra added one more item to her exhaustive list, *she had to trust God with her tears too*. She exhaled, exhausted.

MOMENTS PASSED, and her tears subsided leaving behind a light sniffle.

They lay in her hospital bed, her head never moving from his chest. Bruce was making soothing circles on her back. He reached for the Kleenex box and grabbed a few and dried her face.

"Here," he folded a couple more into her hand, "before you decide to wipe your boogers on my good shirt."

She leaned back looking into his eyes.

Uncontrollable laughter filled the cold room. Sandra laughed so hard her side ached.

"Boy, leave it to you to say something about boogers."

They burst into laughter again. A nurse poked her head in wondering if all was well.

It was.

Sandra shifted around on the mattress and snuggled back next to him absorbing his warmth.

"One day," Bruce whispered, "you will see everything you need, He has provided. You just have to look in the right place."

Sandra pulled away and searched Bruce's soft brown eyes for the hidden meaning behind his words. "What are you talking about?"

Bruce leaned closer and gazed down into her eyes. He cupped Sandra's face with both hands, longing flickered in his eyes, "Sandi, I—"

"Hey, girl how—" Serafine barged into the room.

HER DECISION

*S*andra felt the distance hanging between them. He was no less attentive, and he was still by her side. But his eyes were bleak as he looked at her.

"Bruce, what is it?"

"What is what?" he responded, turning his eyes to help her into the truck.

Dr. Charles released Sandra from the hospital with strict instructions to stay in bed until her doctor's appointment in a few days. Serafine walked in and whatever he had to say went unsaid.

Bruce tossed her purse in the back and bent to lift her from the wheelchair.

"Oh no, you don't." She said holding up her hand to stop him. "And have you blaming me for a hernia."

"Girl, hush," Bruce said picking her up. One minute she was resisting, the next she was cradled in his arms. "You were saying," he teased.

Sandra felt her chest tighten, she was holding her breath again, and it had nothing to do with her anxious heart. He'd held her before but that time felt more intimate.

"Nothing," she whispered softer than she intended.

He gently placed her in the truck and waited as Sandra fastened her seat belt. The nurse pulled the chair back. She too seemed flustered by his little display.

Bruce closed the door and talked to the nurse. She pointed to the white note with the prescription. He nodded, and Sandra decided to lean back and let him handle it.

Sandra reached for her purse and called Serafine. She explained the doctor's orders to get rest. Sandra would return home with Bruce as her escort. But first, she had to get her stuff from the cabin.

Minutes later Bruce was behind the wheel. He adjusted the seat to accommodate his longer legs.

"Let's get this show on the road." He turned towards Loving Ranch, and Sandra closed her eyes and enjoyed the ride.

"BABY," Bruce lightly shook Sandra awake. "We're here."

She looked out the window and saw Serafine and the ladies outside the truck. Sandra sat up trying to fix her wrinkled clothes.

"You look beautiful." He said as she pulled down the mirror and snapped it closed.

"I'm not sure I can trust your judgment. Look at

these bags under my eyes." Sandra smoothed her hands over her two-stranded twists.

Bruce chuckled as he got out the truck and opened her door. He helped her down and stepped back to give the women room.

Sandra was enclosed by the women, as they hugged and doted on her. She felt overwhelmed with their love and concern for her wellbeing. Miss Abby had become a close companion while at the retreat and she stood back until the other ladies finished. Finally, she stepped forward.

"You scared me, young lady!" She said pulling Sandra into a tight motherly hug.

"I'm sorry. It wasn't intentional." Sandra accepted the love and knew she had made a forever friend in Miss Abby.

They stood holding each a while before Miss Abby asked, "So who is this fine young thang?" She winked at Bruce.

He smiled blushing, showing all the beautiful white teeth.

The ladies laughed, "Leave it to you Miss Abby," someone said.

"This is Bruce," Sandra introduced him.

Bruce stepped forward extending his hand, and the two began talking.

Sandra slipped away, she had to pack her belongings in the cabin, Serafine looped their arms together as they walked to the cabin.

"Serafine, I have to return home, but I would like to come back if that is okay with you."

They stopped on the porch.

"I would love to have you. What do you have in mind?"

"I gave a lot of thought to what you said about trusting God. And I've decided I am going to do it. Sitting in that hospital bed scared me straight. I have too much life to live," she paused sitting on the bed. "I'm not sure I fully get it. But I'm hoping I can return and work with you. Maybe an extended stay after the wedding."

"I look forward to it and I'll save your cabin too. But are you sure your up to planning the wedding."

"I think so. I'm going to finish what I started. I also need to talk with my broker about selling my cafe."

"My home is your home. You can stay as long as you like."

They hugged. The two talked finalizing Sandra's return as she packed.

"You all ready Sandi?" Bruce said looking through the screen door.

"I think so."

He stepped in and grabbed her bags. They followed.

"I love you girl but don't take offense, I think I'll miss your trees and my hammock more than anything else."

Serafine smiled, "No offense taken."

They hugged and said their goodbyes. Bruce helped Sandra into the SUV.

～

BRUCE CLOSED THE DOOR. He turned to Serafine and hugged her.

"Thank you for taking care of her," Serafine said before releasing him.

"Always," he responded with a smile.

Bruce stepped back to walk away, but Serafine stayed him with a hand placed gently on his forearm.

Serafine searched his eyes and smiled.

They walked as he turned to round the back she asked, "You love her don't you?"

Bruce froze. He glanced over his shoulder.

"She can't hear us," Serafine confirmed. He looked uncomfortable to her. "Your response is safe with me."

"Yes."

"Why don't you tell her?"

He shrugged, "I will when the time is right. But what she needs most, right now, is a friend."

"What do you know about 1 Corinthians 13?"

For the next few minutes, Serafine explained love as declared in the Bible. He listens and nodded. He hugged her once more, and before getting in the SUV Serafine said, "See you at the wedding."

Serafine watched them drive off. Praying for their safe return and Bruce's strength and courage as he pursued Sandra's heart. But she knew love always won in the end. Something told her Sandra was going to get a run for her money.

Realizing they were out of sight, she chuckled and headed back to the rest of the ladies in the center. She couldn't wait for the wedding. Maybe there'd be not one bride but two.

EPILOGUE

Four months later...

"Were those pickles I saw in the kitchen?" Bruce asked coming up behind Sandra rubbing her shoulders.

She rolled her neck giving him full access to her tight shoulders. "Yes, what do you expect from a pregnant bride?"

They laughed. Bruce folded Sandra's hand in his and escorted her to the dance floor. She followed without question.

Bruce pulled her into his arms as the slow danced. Sandra laid her tired head on his chest and let him sing to her as they blocked out the world.

Sandra was truly happy for her sister. She was a gorgeous bride and was sure her new brother-in-law, Russell, would have his hands full with Cindy and the babies.

"Oh brother, why are you crying now?" Bruce asked wiping her tears away.

"Oh, hush...," she playfully hit his chest, leaned back looking into his eyes, "Wasn't she beautiful?"

"Yes, she was," he agreed.

They danced, and Sandra heard, "Son." She turned and smiled as her father extended an air toast in their direction.

"Yes, sir," Bruce responded. "I think your pops is drunk."

They laughed until Sandra's eyeliner and mascara were all over his white dress shirt.

"Daddy always liked you," Sandra said when she could talk without laughing at her father's glassy eyes.

"The feeling is mutual," Bruce said resting his cheek on her head.

Moments later, Cindy threw the bouquet, and it landed in Sandra's lap. Sandra laughed it off twirling it in the air.

Cindy claps with glee, "You're next big sis!"

SANDRA COLLAPSED into the first chair she saw. She did it. The wedding went without a hitch, and she was free. She felt accomplished.

Her scare at Loving Ranch was the kick in the butt she needed. She returned home and immediately went about getting her life in order. Starting with Cindy and her rushed wedding. They agreed to change the date if she wanted Sandra's help. Cindy also deferred to her choices through the planning process to keep the peace.

Sandra heard clapping and howling and turned in the direction of the noise. It was Bruce. She bowed.

"It is finished. And in grand style. How are you?"

"Never better, except my feet. Fashion can be brutal," Sandra said holding up her stilettos.

"You looked good in them," he said with a boyish smile.

"Why, thank you, sir," she returned the smile tossing her shoes to the floor.

"Now, give me these hushpuppies. Tell me about this 'never better.'"

Bruce sat across from her, placing her feet in his lap. He started rubbing the ball of her foot with his thumb.

"I think I've done something right in this world," she joked as he rubbed her aches and pains away.

The staff moved around cleaning the dining hall. Sandra saw Cindy off on their honeymoon, sent her parents in a limo with a driver, and now she sat sipping a glass of champagne with a foot rub. She would head back to Loving Ranch, and her attorney found a buyer for her cafe.

Her life was looking up. She recalled words from Serafine, "All good things come from the Lord."

Her heart whispered, *Thank you Father*.

BRUCE STAYED with her as she paid the caterer and returned the keys to the hall manager. He walked

Sandra to her SUV. He reached for the door handle and stopped.

He turned and searched her eyes.

"What is it?" Sandra reached for Bruce's hand.

Her move towards him seemed to be the answer he needed. Bruce cupped her face between her hands and lowered his head towards her. He paused, and she leaned closer.

Bruce kissed her softly with slow precision. He cradled the back of her head and pulled their bodies together deepening the kiss before resting his forehead on hers. Both breathing heavily.

What just happened? Sandra's entire body vibrated to the thump of her heart. Bruce had kissed her and everything about him called to everything within her, she hadn't seen it coming.

"Sandi, come and spend a few weeks with me in Atlanta?" The words rushed out as he pressed her close.

Sandra looked up and saw the vulnerability in his eyes and answered just as quick, "Yes."

His arms tightened around her, "Thank you, love, thank you."

Sandra smiled because she saw in his eyes what she desired most, *love*.

Did you enjoy *Love's Hope*?

Reviews are important; you can help me by writing even a short one.

Is love worth risking their friendship? Read what happens when Bruce invites Sandra on an exotic vacation. (Two chapters are coming up just click forward to start reading.)

Thank you so much! Take care and I hope to "see" you soon.

   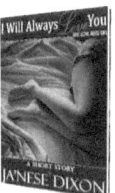

You're Invited to…*Reader's Staycation*, my newsletter.

New subscribers get four (*YES four!*) short stories of various lengths as my gift for joining. And don't worry, I don't send them all at once, but spread them out.

Each story will come with a little insight into why I wrote it and most take less than 30 minutes to read.

After the first month, I'll send monthly updates with new releases, book reviews, current contests, giveaways and book-related news.

Join and get YOUR free stories!

http://www.jansedixon.com/newsletter

Sandra James, owner of Coffee Confessions, a small Houston coffee shop that serves up coffee, books, music and good ole' fashion customer service, which keeps her shop full of eclectic patrons at the cost of her personal life. She yearns for a man of her own, but will all hell break loose when a love lost and love anew collide?

Get Your Copy!

CHAPTER 1

"I give," Sandra James whispered to herself in resignation as she locked the doors to Coffee Confessions.

She turned the key until she heard the click. She slid the keys into her apron, grabbed both handles and gave the door a good shake before allowing the dimly lit shop to consume her thoughts. She watched as the downtown scene outside the shop windows changed from highly paid professionals to easygoing partiers.

An attractive couple snuggled together strolling down the sidewalk caused her to pause mid-stride. She noticed the protective hold he had around the woman's waist and then his hand fell to grip her full hips. The intimacy in the way he held her made Sandra almost too embarrassed to watch. Her mind danced with the same questions that haunted her more often than not. *Was she wrong to want that type of affection in her life? Was it too much to want to share her personal time with another?*

She knew her home away from home was all-consuming, but she had an excellent staff and wonderful patrons, which meant she could make time for that special someone if she could find someone worth giving her time.

Sandra continued walking and gave a parting look towards the couple as they disappeared into the night, leaving a quiet yearning within her.

She glanced at her watch, noticing the time; it was almost eleven o'clock. Out of nowhere, an unladylike yawn escaped. Sandra tried to hide it behind the back of her hand as she looked from side-to-side, locking eyes with Bruce Daniels. They shared a gut tightening laugh as she grabbed a damp towel and continued cleaning the tables. She would push her relationship woes to the side, *for now.*

Most nights Bruce closed the shop with her. He was an up-and-coming producer who started working for her over five years ago as a college student. Over the years their relationship had morphed into a good friendship. Their conversations flowed when they found themselves alone. It was inevitable.

What she found refreshing about their relationship was that there were no strings attached, it was strictly platonic. It was good for her spirit and nice to get the thoughts of a handsome, eligible man.

"What do you give on, Sandi? Life or just tonight?" Bruce's eyes swept the length of her body as he sat casually perched on the edge of the table, legs crossed at the ankles.

Sandra lowered her body to the closest chair,

thinking about his question, knowing she could hide nothing from him. She played with a lock of hair before pushing it behind her ear. The room stood quiet. As he waited, she heard the laughter and chatter of a small crowd passing the shop. A light tap on the glass cut through the stillness. Sandra noticed a young woman in a midriff-revealing outfit staring openly at Bruce giving him a finger wave. He nodded sending the group into a fit of giggles. He focused again on Sandra, silently dismissing the young partygoers.

He stood and held up a finger. "Hold that thought. Whatcha drinking, Miss Lady?" Bruce jogged to the service counter. She turned in her chair and watched him get comfortable. He stretched his arms at both sides and shook them as if relieving the tension; he then pushed back his sleeves. She was sure that he could handle the espresso machine with his eyes closed. He grabbed a couple of to-go cups and flipped on the machine.

"I'll take a latte."

"Ahh, come on, Sandi add a little somethin', somethin' to it. What about vanilla or almond?" He suggested a couple of flavors to dress up her milk filled coffee. Bruce shrugged his shoulders, giving her his best smile, showing all the pearly-white teeth God gave him.

His power of persuasion was not working. Sandra shook her head and turned her nose up, resembling a two-year-old refusing to eat spinach. He grabbed his chest as if heartbroken and she leaned into the table, laughing.

"How can you own the best coffee shop in Houston and still drink plain ole' lattes?"

Sandra folded the damp towel into a neat square, smiling at the thought. "You know I love coffee. It's always been about the coffee. I love the smell, the taste, and the soothing way it goes down."

He threw up his hands in surrender, "Alright, alright. Latte it is."

Bruce moved about, making their drinks. She wondered how long she could expect him to stick around? He was her right-hand man, and she trusted him more than once with running the shop in her absence. She knew her role as his boss would end soon as his popularity in the music industry increased. Her little paychecks were mere chump change against the thousands he was receiving for his work with local artists.

Sandra felt a gloomy mood lingering over her. She would miss his zany energy and the way he kept her laughing. "I heard your latest song with Marques on the radio today."

"What did you think?" His head snapped up waiting for her assessment.

Sandra knew his growing popularity on the radio did not curb his anxiety since he knew the music industry could be fickle. She thought his misgivings were ridiculous, however, parts of her understood since she'd been there when she decided to open Coffee Confessions. Everyone thought she was foolish for not pursuing a corporate gig after receiving her MBA. But she was sold after working at the campus coffee shop, and during graduate school, she began writing her business plan to open her own shop.

Sandra loved connecting with people. She would sit back watching them relax while taking pleasure in drinking her coffee. It was like personally inviting them into her home. Life taught her, on more than one occasion, that anything and everything could be solved over a good cup of coffee.

"Was it that bad?" Sandra looked into his eyes and read his misgivings.

"Are you crazy? I loved it. I'm sorry I got lost in my thoughts. I have a feeling I'm going to lose you soon."

He sat their cups on the table, a deep crease forming between his full brows. She wrapped her hands around the cup finding comfort in its warmth.

"Are you trying to get rid of me?" Things are going good, but I don't plan to quit my day job until I see more zeros on my checks. Besides, I won't leave you hanging; I want to make sure you have a solid replacement."

"Well, they're coming. I'd bet my shop on it. And don't worry about me, I'm a big girl."

They chatted about the shop and her current employees. She may have to place an ad in the paper and start interviewing soon.

"So, what's up with you? You seemed out of it tonight."

Sandra crossed her legs and leaned closer to the table. She could smell the cinnamon rising from his cup. She relaxed and placed her chin in the palm of her hand.

"I feel like I don't have much of a life. I'm here from sun up to sun down. And I'm not complaining because I love my business, but I always thought I would have kids by now and I don't even have a man." She fell back in the chair, crossing her arms in her lap.

"Girl, you act like you're a hundred years old. It's not too late." He took a drink of his coffee. "How about I set you up with someone?"

Sandra lifted her hands in protest, "Oh, no, no, no… I am not turning into a charity case."

"Whatever."

Bruce dismissed her response, and she could see the wheels in his head turning. She had to stop him. Sandra could just imagine some kid, strolling in with his pants hanging to the floor, showing his expensive drawers to the world, and Lord help her if he showed up with a mouth full of fancy hardware. She was too old for that. She needed a nice, respectable guy. The problem was, *how would she find him*?

"Earth to Sandi," Bruce snapped his fingers to regain her attention.

"You know what, thanks, but no thanks. I don't think I'm the young hip-hop kind of woman. I need a nice settled man." Her list of qualities for her ideal man was short. He had to love her independence, her hectic work schedule, her family, and most importantly, her girls.

"Dang! Don't you trust your boy? I got you. Give me a chance."

Sandra paused. Bruce plastered a smile on his face and her stomach twisted into a knot. She knew she had to try, but something whispered, *Brace yourself.* Her thirty-fifth birthday was months away, and things would remain the same if she didn't at least try.

"Okay, I'll give you a chance. But I don't want a—"

He held up his hand, cutting off her impending checklist. "No, thanks. I got this."

Sandra picked up her cup and drained it. She couldn't believe Bruce was playing matchmaker and setting her up on a blind date. She stood to throw her cup in the trash but slumped back into her still warm chair upon realizing she didn't know any of his friends outside the shop. He could find her some crazed lunatic.

"Actually, I don't know if this is a good idea," she said, her voice just above a whisper.

"I know the kind of guys you like." He leaned back in the chair and assessed her. She squirmed under his watchful eye. "You like those conservative, educated, I want to take you to a jazz club kinda dudes." Bruce laughed, but the nervous knot in her stomach prevented her from joining him.

"Sandi, I got you. Really. I have someone that's perfect. Let's get through having Marques here this weekend, and I'll set something up for next week."

Bruce stood, and she did too. He grabbed their cups and started gathering the trash. It was past midnight, and he was probably headed to the studio. She planned to go straight home and pray. She knew without a doubt that she trusted him with her business, but *could she trust Bruce with finding her a date*?

He strolled around the coffee shop while she

adjusted the chairs and placed the random books left around the shop back on the bookshelves. Bruce was a catch, and he knew it. He stood over six feet, and his body showed the results of spending many hours in the gym. However, he had a jealous mistress—his music.

He lived, slept, and had all but married his music career. Sandra knew he stayed around Coffee Confessions because it was easy and he still had most of the day to himself. His salary had afforded him studio time in the beginning and then music equipment. As a result, he created beats, wrote songs, and produced several genres of music.

She walked to the back office and grabbed her things. She slung her purse across her body, resolving that one date wouldn't kill her. Besides she would talk it over tomorrow with her girls at their monthly lunch. They kept it real, and she hoped a pep talk from them would settle her nerves.

She stood at the door, locking eyes with Bruce as he casually walked in her direction. His reassuring smile did not lessen the tension flowing through her body. She knew it was too late to drink coffee, but Sandra knew her anxious nerves had nothing to do with that and everything to do with jumping back into the dating scene.

Lord help her.

CHAPTER 2

*S*andra was a born and bred Houstonian. She didn't wear cowboy boots or a cowgirl hat; it wasn't her style. The thought made her chuckle. She loved Houston, and she could line dance with the best of them. And one day she would be laid to rest in Texas soil, and that made her who she was—proud, dedicated, and determined.

She treated people with respect and in return, she demanded the same. She was self-made, well not totally, her family supported her every whim and dream. Coffee Confessions was just one of her dreams come true.

Sandra entered the cafe, greeting a few of her regular morning customers. Sleep evaded her last night and thoughts of her upcoming date had her nerves on end. She started the day with a renewed determination; she would find someone to love. Having a man with a potential for children would add icing on top of her already decadent cake called life.

It was Friday, which was always busy, plus she had to prepare for the flood of women expected for Saturday's live showcase with Marques. They served everything from house drip coffee to fancy six-dollar concoctions. But where her cafe differed from the others was the small bookstore offering the best in indie books, and she built an intimate environment for live music. Bruce's inside connection with up-and-coming artists bode well for the cafe. She now booked artists nearly a year in advance for private shows. They came to test new music or to have an intimate concert where they could literally touch their fans.

Sandra walked to her small office. She tossed her purse in the bottom drawer of her desk and pressed the power button. She waited as it powered up taking several deep breaths in preparation for the day ahead. Sandra grabbed her shoulder length locks and tied them in a functional knot while scanning her desk for something mellow. Satisfied when she located Maxwell's new CD, she popped it in and clicked play. She began her daily ritual of reviewing the books and calling for her weekly fresh deliveries of sandwiches and homemade pastries. She loved being able to patron locally-owned businesses. She'd worked several hours when she paused to buzz the service counter.

"Hey, Valencia," she glanced at the handcrafted clock on her wall noticing the time, "my sisters are coming in about a half hour. Have a table reserved and our regular selections prepared."

Valencia's eagerness and upbeat spirit made the customers love her. The young woman had some issues with her family, but she'd caught on quickly and made everyone around her work harder. Sandra only needed to ask once, and Valencia made it happen. She kept people around her that needed little supervision since she believed in giving her employees room to grow. In her five years of business, the formula worked because she'd never fired anyone. All of her old employees left to pursue other aspirations or to follow their personal goals, but never due to unhappiness with their job.

Sandra's thoughts drifted back to Bruce. He would one day be compared to Quincy Jones or the Timberland's of the industry, and when that day came, she would miss him. A couple of years ago she'd approached him about increasing the caliber of artist they featured in what she'd dubbed *Midnight Confessions*. She closed the shop as normal, and the ticketed showcase ran for a few hours. The customers loved it, and she'd noticed the increased patronage from area celebrities and athletes. Her hard work was finally showing in both her business and personal bank accounts. She wasn't doing too badly for a small business, especially against the industry giants. She'd carved out a unique place in Houston. Now all she wanted to do was transfer her efforts from her business to her personal life.

Lost in a daydream, Sandra was startled back to reality by the ringing of the shop phone. She required answering the phone within two rings. Ringing phones were annoying, and many people used her establishment as a getaway. They read, studied, talked, but very few people chatted on cell phones because it felt unnatural in the surroundings. She did her best to keep that vibe. She stood up to leave the office, but when she realized she wouldn't make it to the front counter in time, she doubled back and snatched the phone off the receiver at the beginning of the third ring.

"Coffee Confessions, give in to your guilty pleasure. This is Sandra, how can I be of service?"

"Damn, it's like that?"

She paused. The warm baritone voice rivaled a late night disc jockey. She chuckled and shook her head at the thought. Ignoring his statement, she asked again, "Is there something I can help you with?"

"I wish," was all she heard.

"Come again?" He was beginning to annoy her. Barry White's sexy double needed to get going, she had things to do. She sat on the end of her desk, leaning slightly forward to see if her girls had arrived.

"You caught me off guard. I almost forgot why I called. You have a sexy voice." She prepared to respond in a not-so-friendly fashion until his rambling cut her short. "I'm sorry. I just realized how rude and sexist I might sound." He laughed. She joined in more out of nervous energy than humor. The sound vibrating through the phone caused her stomach to tighten. She couldn't help but respond to his electric vibe transmitting through the phone.

"Forgiven." Sandra waited for him to state the reason for his call.

"Is Bruce available?" The moment dissipated into formality.

"No, he's not. I can take a message." Sandra grabbed a pencil and prepared to take the message.

"Yes, please tell him to call Ricardo. He's expecting me in town tomorrow, but I arrived early. I called his cell phone, but I'm assuming he's still sleeping because I haven't heard from him."

"I'll pass the message along. Is there anything else I can help you with today?" She passively asked while jotting down the message on a notepad.

"No, not unless you want me to embarrass myself further."

She could hear the smile in his voice and giggled at his discomfort. "Please don't. I'll give it to him. Thank you for calling Coffee Confessions."

Sandra hung up and wondered whether his face matched his voice as a small shiver pulsed through her. She could still hear the richness of his tone. She needed to find a date because here she was trying to drum up an image of a potential customer. If she weren't careful, she would morph into a desperate old hag.

"Miss Sandra, the ladies are here."

Valencia walked into her office and announced the arrival of her sisters. Sandra felt her brief melancholy lift as she nearly knocked Valencia over and barreled through the shop, closing in on the rowdy bunch that was busy flirting with a group of men across the room. They appeared to enjoy the attention because they were all smiles.

Sandra placed her hand on her hip and shook her

head at Alicia, Danyelle and Faith snickering like schoolgirls. As she suspected, Danyelle was the ringleader of the flirting session.

She and Danyelle had been friends longer than she could remember. They'd met while in grade school. Faith joined the duo a few years later, and they officially became a quartet when the three of them became friends with Alicia in college.

Sandra talked to them individually several times a week. However, they found it harder to stay in touch as their personal obligations grew, so they vowed to meet monthly for a sisters' circle. They laughed, talked, cried, and relieved the weight of their problems, drawing strength from each other. They kept it real and knew no limits to protecting each other whether the source was a friend or foe. As a result, each woman usually left the shop with a new pep in her step and ready to take on the world once again.

"Don't shake your head at me," Danyelle said, standing to hug Sandra.

"Someone should tame this crazy woman." Sandra laughed and held her friend tight. "Besides, you already have a man."

"Whatever! I'm like Beyoncé, if he wants it, he betta put a ring on it. Until then, I'm a free agent." Danyelle said, taking her seat.

The women erupted into a chorus of laughter, exchanging welcoming hugs and clearing the table for their lunch. As if on cue, Valencia approached the table with their sandwiches, fruit, and sweet tea. Sandra didn't require her to act as a server, but Valencia jumped at the chance since the ladies tipped her generously. She could easily make one hundred dollars in tips from the bunch.

"Oh no, what has Steve done now?" Alicia turned her worried expression to Danyelle. Alicia lived a fairytale life. She and her husband lived in River Oaks and had a son. She was the mother hen of the crew, and she wore her badge well.

"What hasn't he done?" Danyelle took a bite of her turkey and Swiss on wheat bread. They waited, knowing Danyelle might be the mouthpiece of the group, but she was tight-lipped when it came to her personal affairs. She crossed her arms on the edge of the table. "Honestly, I'm tired of waiting for Steve to propose. We've been together for seven years. I'm no different than the next woman. I want to have the house, kids, and the dog."

They nodded in unison.

"I have a house, my business is thriving, I have a man that I love, what is he waiting on? *Jesus*!"

A forced smile failed to disguise the hurt in her tear-filled eyes. She searched their faces as if they held the answers to the issues plaguing her heart. Sandra grabbed Danyelle's hand and squeezed it, knowing exactly how she felt.

Faith watched as they comforted Danyelle. She rarely showed her emotions, but she took personal offense to anyone causing harm to her sisters. "Why do you have to wait on him, Danyelle? He's not the only eligible person in Houston."

Sandra exchanged a look with Alicia, noticing

Faith's use of "person" instead of "man." Alicia impassively shrugged her shoulder.

Danyelle patted her eyes with the tissue, careful not to smudge her eyeliner. "Why? Because I be damned if I wasted seven years of my life? Besides, I love him. We live together. And why should I not want him to man up and ask me to marry him?" With every word, the tears were forming in her eyes, threatening to spill over again.

Sandra knew this was serious. She could not remember the last time she saw Danyelle cry. Faith looked like she could strangle Steve with her bare hands and Alicia was Alicia, trying to soothe everyone.

"Well," Sandra said, trying to lighten the mood, "guess who's going on a blind date next week?" She swore she could hear a pin drop.

"Oh goodness, Sandra, when are you going to start serving liquor?" Faith asked sending them all into a fit of laughter. They laughed until tears streamed down their perfectly made up faces. Alicia doubled over holding her stomach and Sandra would have been offended if their reaction to her going on a blind date wasn't hysterical.

They took a moment to get their emotions under control. "Okay, start at the beginning," Alicia coaxed. She sat back in her seat, letting Valencia refill their glasses of tea and placed a plate of chocolate chip cookies on the table. They huddled closer, each grabbing a cookie.

Sandra nodded, breaking a piece of the soft cookie

and popping it into her mouth. "Last night Bruce asked if he could set me up with one of his friends."

"Bruce?" They asked in unison.

"Shoot, I would love to do something to his fine ass," Danyelle mumbled.

Alicia's saucer-sized eyes caused the women to fill the shop with their laughter again. The more perturbed the other guests appeared, the more they laughed. Danyelle looked at everyone; her stern expression dared them to say something. After the laughter had subsided, Sandra pleaded, "Stop, I'm going to give this a chance. I warned him. I don't want some young, thug-wanna-be guy. He said he knows, and I trust him."

"Mmmmhm." Faith said, sarcastically.

Sandra ignored her. After listening to today's conversation, she planned to take it with a grain of salt. She would try.

Alicia's expression twisted in thought. "I think you should. When was the last time you went on a date before Noah quit his job to build the ark?" They all but rolled on the floor at Alicia's wisecrack.

"Girl, you know it's been so long that her coochie is probably full of dust."

Uncontrollable laughter filled the shop once more. Sandra tried to stop, but she knew Danyelle was right. She saw Valencia looking on at the rambunctious bunch disrupting the calm of the shop, and she saw a flash of something in her eyes. *Was it envy*? Before she could name it, it disappeared.

Sandra threw a napkin at Danyelle, who ducked, bumping into Faith.

"No really, all jokes aside, I think you should. Actually...I have an idea." They all sobered and gathered closer as if Alicia had a naughty secret.

"Oh, hell. Why do I feel like I'm being set up?" Sandra watched her friend's eyes dance like a mischievous child.

"Because you are." Alicia's rubbed her hands together like Brain preparing to take over the world. "At our next sister's circle, I'm bringing a plan for us. I think we should get our men and woman," she said in Faith's direction, "in check."

"Please, just say I don't have to rub noses with your husband's bougie friends." Faith moaned.

"No, it's nothing like that." Alicia laughed.

They had weathered many formal affairs to support Alicia, and she knew they would do anything she asked.

"And can we please move the meeting to a place that serves something harder than sweet tea? No offense, Sandi." Danyelle asked.

"None taken."

"Okay, okay. Let's meet at Grooves or something like that." Alicia suggested.

"Wait, the next sister's circle? You guys are coming tomorrow, right?" Sandra asked.

"Hell yeah! I wouldn't miss Marques' for nothing. Do you think he'll take off his shirt? In his latest video, he had me wishing I was that video girl." Danyelle could go from hot to cold in an instant. She sat in her chair rolling her body like a true video vixen. A party wasn't a party without her.

"I wish you would stop. And don't embarrass me." Sandra said before whispering behind her hand, "I hope so too."

After chatting for another half hour, the ladies stood and prepared to leave. Sandra eyed the cash left on the table, and sure enough, Valencia would be happy. They all wished her well and agreed that she should go on the blind date.

Sandra stood on the sidewalk waving her goodbyes as her friends walked away. She knew they would have a great time at the show tomorrow. She could not help but wonder what Alicia had up her sleeve and what was going on in Danyelle's life. *Time would tell*, she reasoned.

Sandra turned to walk into the shop and heard, "Hey good lookin', can I get those digits?"

"Did you enjoy this exclusive excerpt from *Caramel Surprise*? **Buy the book**. I hope to see you again, otherwise it was a pleasure to meet you. Take care!

Is love worth risking their friendship?

He's in love with his best friend, and she doesn't know it.

Bruce exudes confidence as a multi-diamond album producer, amassing wealth, and enough toys to keep all eyes on him. He is on the cusp of another major life transition, and he can't imagine pursuing it without Sandra by his side.

Sandra is rebuilding her life after a health scare. A life she hoped would include love, however, she's quite certain she's experienced more heartbreak than one heart should ever endure. But she can't stop daydreaming about a stolen kiss they once shared.

Bruce is secretly in love with Sandra and he's ready to get his woman.

Sandra reluctantly agrees to accompany Bruce for an exotic getaway. He will have seven days to convince her, he desires more than friendship, *he wants forever*.

Journey to paradise as Bruce and Sandra discover....*whether love is worth risking their friendship.*

Get Your Copy!

INCOMPLETE

"*D*o you trust me Sandra?" Bruce Daniels made a wise decision of making his request by video because, for this discussion, he needed to see Sandra's face.

Her eyes filled with unease at the question, and her ebony twists pulled back in a ponytail he had an unobstructed view of the guarded expression on her makeup-free face. Still, he would not take no for an answer.

Sandra lower to the cardinal couch and moved a pillow to support her lower back. "What do you mean? You know I trust you, but that's a loaded question. And stop with that silly smile. What are you up to?"

Bruce was about to orchestrate the biggest undertaking of his life. He hoped it ended with Sandra James as his fiancé.

"I need your help."

"Whatcha got kiddo?"

He hoped she didn't see him cringe. That was part of their issue. Sandra saw him as just a friend. Bruce wanted to be more than friends, and everyone knew it but her.

Patience, he chided his runaway heart.

He had a plan and when it was all said and done she would no longer see him as her best friend, her ride-or-die, or her pal. She would see him as a man, her future husband and, Lord willing, the father of their children. He wanted to give her a lifetime of happiness, and much more, however, their happily-ever-after would be impossible with him in the friend zone.

"I am chaperoning Marques to an industry event, and I need a date." There he said it.

"Your date?" Her eyes bucked in surprise and she started to nibble on her lower lip.

"Yes, Sandra, my date."

His eyes watched her. The best part of their seven-year friendship was he knew her. Sandra was a processor, and she couldn't be pushed into a decision. He'd give her the space needed to consider his request, because she had to be willing, but he would not allow her room to overthink it.

"I don't know if that's a good idea," a sudden look of apprehension passed across her clouded face.

"So you're not going to help me?" He steeled his facial expressions and leaned back as his plan take its course. Sandra would go to the end to help a friend. It was in her DNA.

"Why do I have to be your date to help you?"

"Because woman, that's what I want. So are you going to do it? Or are you turning me down?" He leveled his gaze. His heart raced, but he couldn't back down. Getting her away from Houston and her normal life was imperative.

"Why are you—"

"5…4…3—"

"Don't you dare start the countdown on me!" She pointed her finger at him letting out an exasperated growl. "And wipe that silly grin off your face."

"We don't have all day. I'll ask you again. Will you join me as my date?"

"No funny business." She demanded.

"I can't make any promises," he stated unbending.

"Bruce!"

"I'm not going to lie to you. But you're always safe with me. I'd never do anything to compromise you or our relationship." And he wouldn't, and that promise had made it harder to pursue her. What if he lost it all trying to gain what he wanted most, *her heart*.

"I know." Her eyes softened. "But we just finalized the sale of the shop and—"

"You have your team handling it. We'll have the internet and full connection. And I can arrange for you to return should an emergency arise. I'm not a begging man, but I'll make this one exception." He had a list of her potential excuses mapped out in his mind. He knew she wouldn't make it easy. "Please Sandi."

"Oh…okay." She seemed unsure.

"Thank you! You won't regret it." Relief washed over him. It was official. Now to get things rolling.

"Where are we going?" She pulled her leg beneath her and rocked a little on the couch before settling back into the plush cushions.

"It's a surprise." He could feel that silly grin on his face again because he felt like he'd won a billion dollar lottery. She said yes. Actually, it was okay, but he'd take it.

"Bruce...," Sandra narrowed her eyes as she searched his face.

"You promised." He planned to milk that promise too. "Don't worry sweet Sandi. You're going to love it."

Sandra rolled her eyes and crossed her arms over her chest. Bruce was ready to show her that they belonged together. They talked for a few more minutes before signing off.

Bruce ended the video call and sat alone in his studio. It took him months to plan this trip, it had to go off without a hitch.

"How'd it go?" Cameron asked from behind him.

"She said yes." Bruce let out the pent up air. He leaned forward resting his forearms on his knees. His mind was running at the speed of lightning considering all he had to do before the trip.

"I knew she would. Let's talk shop."

Bruce stood and followed Cameron out of the studio. They rounded the corner and walked to his office bypassing boxes and movers. The trip would serve his personal and professional needs, but it came in the middle of a major transition for his team. They were weeks away from announcing the launch of Star Status Entertainment. But Bruce wanted his ring on Sandra's finger before the official announcement reached the press.

Bruce stopped at his assistant's desk. "Eliana have the package delivered."

"Yes, sir." She reached for the phone and a smile lit up her face. "I'm so excited for you."

"Me too. But this is just the beginning. Let me know if you hit any snags."

"Will do."

Bruce entered his office and settled behind his desk. His office was full of boxes. His awards, plaques, and industry accolades were carefully packed. It took him five years to make it all happen and then he recognized a window of opportunity. He only hoped it would all work out for their good.

"Man, stop daydreaming." Cameron interrupted his musing.

Bruce nodded giving Cameron his undivided attention.

"The arrangements for the showcase and pre-launch weekend are here."

Cameron passed a short stack of papers to Bruce affixed with a staple. Bruce flipped the pages, scanning the contents. He approved the itinerary, guest list, and the budget. The week was costing them a little under a million dollars. The festivities would help them gauge the media's reaction to their artists and launch Star Status Entertainment in style.

"When should I expect you?" Bruce asked not

looking up. Cameron would remain in Atlanta to oversee the movers before flying out.

"I'll make it by mid-week to relieve you." Cameron leaned back in the chair and assessed Bruce. "Are you sure about this?"

Bruce locked eyes with Cameron—his childhood friend. They were friends in the womb. Their families vacationed, holidayed, and raised their children together. He was the brother Bruce didn't have. "Sure about what? SSE?"

"No, Sandra."

Bruce dropped the papers on the oversized executive desk and faced Cameron head-on.

"We have a lot riding on this launch, and we can't afford for you to get distracted."

"I told you, I'm not signing without doing this first." They'd rehashed this argument for the last month. Bruce wasn't budging so Cameron might as well give it up.

"You have a million women hanging on your every beat."

"All I want is her."

Cameron shook his head in resignation, "You were always a hardheaded one."

"Not hardheaded, persistent."

"Yeah, whatever," he gave a gruff laugh. "Just tell her who you are, and you'll know if she's in it for the long haul."

"No." People changed once they knew the identity of his parents. It was easier as the man behind the music. Deciding to start SSE meant he couldn't hide in the shadows anymore. He would be thrust into the limelight, whether he wanted it or not. Bruce couldn't risk scaring Sandra off. He had to tell her on his own terms. "I told you none of this is final until I handle this, and you agreed."

Cameron held up his hands in surrender. "Man, I got your back, and I'll propose to her myself if it means you'll be happy. I'll back off, for now."

Bruce watched Cameron leave knowing he meant well. This time Bruce would have it his way or not at all.

He closed his eyes and let his head fall back. A part of him understood Cameron's concern. But he didn't know Sandra. She was a light of life and the driving force behind every goal he'd achieved as a producer. He would prove to her that he could love her, support her, and protect her. Now he had to trust that he'd done all he could to convince her. His life was his offering and evidence of his love for her.

The most disturbing part was the uncertainty. Was it worth risking their friendship? He couldn't imagine not having her in his life. *But what about the shop?* Bruce pushed aside the internal whisper and chose to trust his plan, confident that it would all work out.

Bruce slipped his hand into his pocket for his constant companion. His fingers glided over the velvet box. He sat it on the edge of his desk and slowly opened it. The fluorescent office lights danced off the diamonds as he stared into the depths of the Cognac brown diamond. The chocolate diamond reminded him of her eyes and the way they first met over coffee.

"She's going to love it," Eliana said entering his office.

Bruce snapped the box closed and placed in back in his pocket. He felt like his entire future hinged on her liking it and loving him the way he loved her.

"I hope we're right."

IT'S COMPLICATED

*S*andra bumped around her house in shock. She was going away with Bruce for a week to an undisclosed location. That called for an emergency sister-friend meeting.

Danyelle, Alicia, and Faith sat around her living room sipping on coffee and tea. Sandra didn't plan to back out of her promise but she was more than nervous, she was petrified.

"I don't know why you're tripping." Danyelle glanced at Sandra over the rim of her mug.

"Tripping? When is the last time you hopped on a plane, or a car, or a boat without knowing the destination." Sandra screeched.

"Baby, I'd follow *that* man to hell and back." Danyelle tipped her mug in a mock salute to Bruce, and their thunderous roars of laughter made Sandra. Danyelle knew how to break up the tension.

"Stop drooling over her man with your crazy self." Faith added.

"He's not my man. We are friends. Strictly friends." Sandra was talking, but no one believed her.

"Mmmmhmmm." The three sang in unison.

"Jinx." Alicia hollered.

"Pinch-poke you owe me a Coke." Faith pinched Danyelle.

"I'm about to pinch-poke you!" Danyelle protested.

They laughed until they cried.

Alicia reached for Sandra's hands. "What is the problem? We all know Bruce cares for you. Do you expect us to believe you don't notice it?"

That was the question of the hour. Sandra saw it, and she tried to ignore it, passing it off. He was just infatuated with his boss or an older woman. However, over the years of talking and hanging out, they had become inseparable and the line holding their friendship intact was blurred.

"I noticed. But I don't want to lose my best friend."

"I'm sorry baby, but women don't stay friends with men like that." Danyelle echoed Sandra's concern. They all sipped on that one. "I think we need to upgrade to some wine."

The doorbell rang.

"I'll get it." Faith sprang to her feet. "And the last thing we need to give your crazy butt is wine."

The robust conversations abruptly stopped when Faith returned with a large decorative box. Her eyes sparkled with excitement.

"Who is it from?" Sandra asked, not expecting a package.

"Guess."

They were all on the edge of the couch in anticipation.

"Bruce," the words were out of her mouth before she could stop them.

Faith nodded.

Sandra opened her arms to accept the box. She walked to the kitchen; she wanted spaced to process it all.

She grabbed a butter knife out of the drawer and cut through the clear packing tape. She took a deep breath and opened the flaps of the box. She sensed the ladies behind her but continued digging through the packing peanuts until her fingertips connected with a hard object. Sandra thrust both hands in and pulled out a royal purple gift box with a silver wire bow.

"Bruce ain't playing." Danyelle teased.

"Shhhh…." Faith and Alicia hissed.

Danyelle rolled her eyes.

"Should we leave you alone?" Alicia asked as Faith moved the large box to the side.

"I ain't going nowhere," Danyelle demanded. Even Sandra had to laugh at that one.

Sandra noticed a card on the outside. *Sweet Sandi….* She traced a fingertip over the greeting. Her heart filled with emotion at the mention of the nickname he gave her. It started as an inside joke that became intimate over the years. Every mention of it now served as another invisible thread stitching them together.

Sandra flipped the card over, and the back was empty. She removed the bow and opened the box appreciating his use of her favorite colors. Inside was a silver envelope. She slid her shaking finger beneath the fold. Who was this Bruce?

Everything about his presentation and attention to detail was not missed by Sandra. She pulled out the card wishing she hadn't called the emergency meeting with her girls, flustered she read it aloud.

Sweet Sandi,
Thank you for agreeing to accompany me on a trip to
paradise. (And yes, it's too late to back out.)
Get ready for a seven-day tropical vacation. Only pack your
necessities the rest will await you at our private destination.
Your dream vacation will begin promptly at six in the
morning. See you soon.
Love always,
Bruce Daniels
P.S. Here's your traveling attire. Enjoy!

SANDRA FELT like her chest would explode from the rapid beating of her heart. She placed the box on the couch to dig deeper until she slowly removed a white spaghetti strap bodycon dress. The howling of the ladies made her blush. The flowy mid-length dress dangled on her index fingers, its sexiness not missed by any of the women.

"I hope you're ready," Alicia whispered in her ear.

"I hope I am too."

Sandra pushed the ladies out a couple of hours later and sat alone with her lovely box and messy thoughts. She wanted to talk with someone but that someone was the crux of the problem.

Bruce was her sounding board, her voice of reason, and she needed his advice on how to handle this "tropical vacation." He knew her too well because his chiding against backing out was correct. But she was a woman of her word. He'd flown to her aid a million times, and she'd be there to help him even if it felt like strings were attached.

Sandra draped the dress over the back of the couch and gathered the coffee mugs. She walked to the kitchen and started the water. She washed the dishes considering the upheaval she called life.

Bruce planned this trip at the worse possible time. The ink was still wet on the contract finalizing the sale of her cafe. She found herself struggling to adjust to no longer being "Sandra James, owner of Coffee Confessions." Who was she now without it? And what would she do next?

She found herself in unchartered territories. Her recent health scare motivated her to release all the things she wrongly used to shape her identity.

Sandra sold her business, dumped her boyfriend, and she played it safe by not committing to anything other than returning to Loving Ranch. That was until Bruce kissed her at her sister's wedding and disrupted all of her plans. Because no matter how hard she tried she couldn't stop thinking about him and his plea for her to spend time with him in Atlanta.

"Girl, snap out of it," she chided herself. "He's just being a really good friend. That's it." She tossed the dishtowel into the water and watched the bubbles float over the sink. She smiled popping a few here and there.

Before the girls left Alicia fell back to talk with her alone, she begged Sandra to be open and hear Bruce out. Sandra wondered what that was all about, but she agreed, deducing it was Alicia being a mother hen and looking out for her.

Sandra walked through her house locking all the windows and watering her plants. Her last chore was to remove all the perishable items from the refrigerator. By the time she showered and snuggled in bed, she resolved in her heart to trust Bruce because he was trustworthy. He was the one man in her life that was consistent. So, she'd go with the flow.

Part of her was thrilled at the thought of sitting back and letting him lead the week. On the other hand, her inner need to control all elements of her life was barking at the whole idea. He had three clear strikes in her book. He was younger, in the music industry, and he was still building his career. None of them pointed to where she was heading in her life seeking marriage, family, and stability.

Sandra tossed and turned. It was nights like this that she'd sit on the phone with Bruce until he had to leave for a studio session. Her pride wouldn't let her call and ask the questions keeping her awake. She would ask his advice on whether she should risk her heart again.

Could she trust him not to leave her in a million unrecognizable pieces? Or better yet, would this trip jeopardize the best friendship she'd ever known?

Sandra reached for her cell phone. Maybe she should call it off. It wasn't worth the risk. *But what if it was?*

She fell back into the bed and stared at the ceiling. She was a big girl and had to make the decision on her own.

Before finally drifting off to sleep the memory of his lips one hers under the stars made her resolved to throw caution to the wind and admitting, even if only to herself, that she wanted Bruce to kiss her again. She wanted to see if the sparks she felt when his lips touched hers were real. And for that, she'd try, one more time.

"Did you enjoy this exclusive excerpt from *Hidden Desire*? **Buy the book**. I hope to see you again, otherwise it was a pleasure to meet you. Take care!

Holidays Ever After

ABOUT THE AUTHOR

Ja'Nese Dixon pens tales of romance in several sub-genres. But her favorites are the ones that manage to keep readers sitting on the edge of their seats lying to themselves about reading "just one more chapter".

Ja'Nese is an avid reader and coffee drinker, who also loves to run, cook, and craft. Her ultimate goal as a writer is to give you a little "staycation" with every story. And she aims to make this present story no exception. Sit back, grab a snack and enjoy.

Ja'Nese calls Houston home with her husband, three kiddos and a four-legged diva dog.

Visit her website at www.janesedixon.com if you enjoy romance, suspense and good stories.

Subscribe to Ja'Nese Newsletter "Reader's Staycation" for reader exclusives, regular giveaways and more.

For more information visit:

www.janesedixon.com
info@janesedixon.com